A madman was terminated, but his wrath remained

A laser cannon, created by a maniac, was pointed menacingly at a nuclear submarine, the USS *Zesus*. The machinery operating the weapon was irreversible.... Unstoppable!

When the death charge was released, two hundred U.S. seamen would perish. International security would be blasted to hell.

Gary Manning faced the control panel. Phoenix Force's Canadian hero hopelessly tried to make sense out of the maze of buttons, switches, knobs....

Despair ripped his voice. "I'll be damned if I know how to stop it!"

Mack Bolan's
PHOENIX FORCE

Mack Bolan's
ABLE TEAM

MACK BOLAN
The Executioner

PHOENIX FORCE

AN EXECUTIONER SERIES

Dragon's Kill

Gar Wilson

A GOLD EAGLE BOOK FROM

WORLDWIDE

TORONTO · NEW YORK · LONDON · PARIS
AMSTERDAM · STOCKHOLM · HAMBURG
ATHENS · MILAN · TOKYO · SYDNEY

First edition September 1983

ISBN 0-373-61307-5

Special thanks and acknowledgment to
William Fieldhouse for his contributions to this work.

Printed in Canada

The yellow Toyota taxicab puled out of Tokyo International Airport's main parking lot. The vehicle was not being driven by a cab driver. The man behind the wheel was actually a lieutenant in the Japanese National Security Organization.

Lieutenant Colonel Thomas Merrill did not know the driver's name, although he was aware of the man's real profession. Merrill, an officer in the United States Army, assigned to the S-1 Department of Intelligence stationed in South Korea, had not come to Japan on leave. He wore a blue civilian suit and striped tie, but he was still on duty for Uncle Sam.

The cab traveled slowly along the freeway in a dense traffic jam. Merrill accepted the inconvenience in stride. He had been in the Orient for sixteen years, and he had learned to deal with the massive crowds and congested traffic. Patience was not only a virtue in the Orient, it was a necessity.

The colonel's square face remained impassive as he stared out the window at the enormous metropolis of Tokyo. Skyscrapers, apartment buildings and factories were everywhere.

Merrill had been to Japan many times before. He had always admired Tokyo for being one of the world's most modern, productive, yet charming spots. Japan combined the old and the new. "Bullet trains," the super-fast monorails, shot across the country. Huge office buildings jutted into the sky, the corporate names of Sanyo, Sony and Honda written on them in English as well as Japanese.

Yet the great pagoda-style castles of Osaka, Himeji and Matsue remained. The magnificent bronze Buddha at Kamakura, the Moss Garden of the Kokodera Temple and a thousand other remnants of ancient Japan were symbols of a civilization and culture that had endured for centuries.

Colonel Merrill's mind, however, was too preoccupied with his mission to appreciate the sights.

Japan's location in the Far East puts it close to several Asian nations that are not on very friendly terms with the United States. The Soviet Union, North Korea, Mainland China and Southeast Asia form an enormous horseshoe around Japan. The Land of the Rising Sun had remained strong and independent of the Communist powers; both Tokyo and Washington were anxious to keep it that way.

Merrill was one of the best cryptographers in the U.S. Army. He had deciphered and translated numerous North Korean and Russian military codes. He had also developed codes for the American Forces in Asia that had baffled the experts in Moscow and Pyongyang. Of course, any code can be broken in time, but Merrill kept altering the cipher patterns with new key numerals and letters. He would occasionally change the codes into new variations, using numbers that were actually chapter and verse numbers from the Bible, or page and paragraph numbers from a book or magazine.

Merrill's mission in Tokyo was to meet with his Japanese counterpart, Colonel Ushiba Kakuei. Together they would create a cryptogram system for Japanese Intelligence that would then be fed into enciphering computers to create enough variations in codes to assist the Nippon security experts for over a year.

The taxicab pulled onto the expressway bridge that extends across the Sumida River. Bridges overlap bridges in Tokyo. Tokyo has more overpasses and underpasses than Chicago. Such designs are necessary in a city with a population of fifteen million people.

Suddenly the driver floored the brake. The unexpected stop jarred Merrill forward. He bounced against the backrest of the front seat and muttered a curse.

"Dozo, shitsurei, Merri-*san,"* the driver apologized. "Excuse, Merri-*san,"* he repeated in broken English. Many Japanese have trouble with the letter L because it is not part of their language.

Merrill looked up and saw a green minibus stalled in their path.

The engine must have broken down, Merrill thought, gazing at the opposite lane where traffic moved past the van and the cab. A column of vehicles soon formed behind the taxi.

"Hell," Merrill muttered.

The rear door of the minibus popped open and two figures dressed in gray overalls and stocking masks appeared at the opening. Merrill saw the tubular shapes of silencers attached to the muzzles of the Czech-made Skorpion machine pistols. The pistols were pointed at the cab.

Half a heartbeat later, the Skorpions spit fire and the windshield of the taxi became a network of spiderwebs as 7.65mm bullets punched through the glass. The driver screamed and clawed at his face, then slumped from view.

Merrill did not have time to react as two more masked assassins sprinted from the bus to the cab. He stared into the muzzle of another silencer-equipped Skorpion. The gunman thrust the weapon through the open window on the driver's side.

Copper-jacketed projectiles coughed from the machine pistol, tearing into Lieutenant Colonel Merrill's chest. The American was too startled by the swiftness of the attack to be frightened, and he died too fast to feel pain. The fourth gunman yanked open the car door and shot Merrill in the side of the head with a Makarov 9mm pistol to make sure their victim was dead.

The assassins jumped into the back of the minibus, which immediately bolted away, leaving a trail of cars trapped behind the cab. Moments later the bus turned off the expressway into the heart of Tokyo. By the time the police found the vehicle abandoned in the Shitamachi District, the assassins had already finished drinking their first bottle of sake in celebration of the success of their mission.

ADMIRAL OLIVER SAMUELS stared through the Plexiglas window on the cabin door of his Huey chopper. He nodded in approval when he saw the USS *Undefeated* waiting in the water below. The great vessel resembled a floating airport. The huge flight deck of the aircraft carrier was large enough to serve as a runway for a U-2 jet and was more than adequate to accommodate the Huey.

"The *Undefeated* is right on time," declared Brigadier General Peter Logan, seated next to Samuels in the cabin of the gunship. "Your boys are pretty good, Admiral."

"The Navy is more or less playing host to this little party, General," Samuels said, smiling.

Some party, the admiral thought. A top-secret conference of American and Japanese military intelligence officers could hardly be called a social event, but it was welcome nonetheless.

Prime Minister Yasuhiro Nakasone was very concerned about Japan's national security. Although they might argue about imports and exports, the U.S. recognized Japan as its strongest ally in the Far East. An opportunity to increase defenses and security was eagerly accepted by the Pentagon.

Admiral Samuels of the Office of Naval Intelligence had met General Logan of Army Intelligence in Okinawa, and the two men had then flown to the rendezvous site in the North Pacific—40 degrees latitude,

150 degrees longitude, just beyond the coastal region known as the Japan Trench. The covert international conference of high-ranking intel personnel would take place beneath the decks of the *Undefeated*.

The Huey hovered nine hundred feet above the green blue sea.

The pilot of the helicopter had made radio contact with the *Undefeated* and received permission to land. The gunship descended slowly, approaching the massive gray vessel. Admiral Samuels gazed down at the ocean and noticed a small sailboat cutting across the waves. Although the craft was heading away from the aircraft carrier, her crew could certainly see the chopper approach.

Probably just pleasure sailors or fishermen, Samuels thought. It was highly unlikely the boat contained enemy agents, since security for the conference had been airtight; only a handful of top intelligence personnel knew about it.

The Bell Huey had been instructed to land on the starboard side of the carrier, on a huge rectangle that was an aircraft elevator. The elevator would lower the chopper belowdecks before anyone set foot outside the gunship. Any attempt to spy on them would be useless.

The chopper gradually descended as it neared the destination. No one inside the Huey saw the white smoke trail of a projectile that streaked from the sailboat. Only a few men aboard the *Undefeated* observed the tiny missile as it rocketed toward the chopper.

Before anyone could even shout in alarm, the projectile smashed into the undercarriage of the gunship. A violent explosion ripped the fuselage apart. The eruption tore off the sponson and its support stud, as well as the sliding doors on both sides of the cabin. Fire burst within the cockpit and virtually every window popped from its frame.

The blast tore into the fuel tank and another explosion followed immediately. The entire gunship was turned into a collection of twisted metal, deformed Plexiglas and charred bits of human bodies. The grisly debris fell to the Pacific while the crew of the *Undefeated* watched in horror.

EIGHT HOURS AFTER the incident occurred, Colonel John Phoenix sat in a conference room at Stony Man headquarters and watched the Bell Huey explode in the sky. His lean face stiffened even though Phoenix was no stranger to such destruction.

Colonel John Phoenix had been born Mack Bolan, but he had become the legend known as The Executioner. Bolan launched thirty-eight campaigns against the Mafia. He succeeded time and time again in chopping down the ranks of the mob. The cannibals of the concrete jungles were beaten by a lone warrior, totally dedicated to stamping out the disease of organized crime.

Mack Bolan was officially dead. "Colonel Phoenix" continued the battle against the twentieth-century barbarians, most notably the KGB.

Hal Brognola turned off the videotape machine. "The video footage was taken by a camera mounted on the bridge of the *Undefeated*," he explained. "Standard equipment for an aircraft carrier."

"What about the enemy vessel?" the Executioner asked as he extracted a pack of cigarettes from his pocket.

"A pleasure craft stolen from a port at Hachinohe a few hours earlier," Brognola replied. "The commander of the *Undefeated* kept his cool and did not order the sailboat blown out of the water. Instead he sent several gunships full of SEALS—men from the Navy's Special Force's division—to try to apprehend the saboteurs. The boat had already been abandoned. They had left behind the Russian RP6 rocket launcher used to shoot down the chopper. Naval intel figures the bastards must have been decked out in frogman gear and jumped overboard after the hit. The SEALS hopped into the sea and searched the area, but the assailants had already vanished."

"They probably had a scuba sled waiting under the water attached to the boat," Phoenix remarked. "Only way they could have gotten away that fast." The big warrior fired a cigarette. "Okay, Hal, you've been calling these guys 'saboteurs' and 'assailants'— everything but terrorists. Why?"

"Because this could be a *direct* act of aggression by the Soviet Union," Brognola replied. "I know the first incident was a classic terrorist-style hit, but this is the second top-level intelligence operation in Japan to be sabotaged in less than a week. And the RP6 is a Soviet-made weapon...."

"Which unfortunately does not prove anything," Phoenix stated. "The Russians supply weapons to many terrorist outfits. This business is too crude for a direct Soviet operation. The Soviets manipulate and control terrorist activity, but they try to avoid direct association."

"Whoever is responsible, we've still got a critical situation," Brognola remarked. "I told you what the ONI and Army Intel told us. They're ninety-eight percent certain about how the saboteurs got their information. If they're right, both American and Japanese security is in jeopardy. I'd like to send you to Japan, Mack," Brognola added, "but you were just there—the authorities are still looking for you." The middle man for the White House and Stony Man Farm looked to Bolan for advice.

"You know as well as I do that there's only one unit of crack antiterrorists in the world who can handle this," Bolan said.

Brognola nodded.

Once again, Phoenix Force was on the verge of some hot action.

2

"Bloody cowards," David McCarter spat. The cold anger in his tone robbed his clipped British accent of its usual charm. He had just watched the videotape of the helicopter being blasted from the sky.

"Courage has never been a favored trait among terrorists," Colonel Yakov Katzenelenbogen commented, fishing a pack of Camels from the pocket of his tweed jacket.

"Then you agree with Colonel Phoenix?" Hal Brognola asked, addressing the four men seated at the same conference table where he had met with Mack Bolan.

Four men: McCarter, the dashing short-tempered Englishman, formerly of the crack SAS commandos; Yakov Katzenelenbogen, the one-armed Israeli, who looked like a college professor, yet was one of the most experienced and competent fighting men in the world; Rafael Encizo, a veteran of the Bay of Pigs invasion, a fiery, fearless Cuban and an expert in underwater warfare; Gary Manning, the Canadian demolitions expert, as strong as a young bull with more endurance than a team of oxen.

All were members of Phoenix Force. They were the

cream of the professional crop, the best antiterrorists in the world. One member, Keio Ohara, was absent from the meeting. Phoenix Force was the American foreign legion, handpicked by Mack Bolan. Like Bolan, they fought fire with fire. Phoenix Force asked no quarter from the international cannibals—and they gave none.

"No doubt about that," Gary Manning answered Brognola's question as he sipped black coffee. "If a MiG fighter jet or a Russian submarine was involved, then we might consider a direct action by the Russians."

"And why attack the helicopter?" Rafael mused, leaning back in his chair. "A missile or two from a MiG or a sub could have destroyed the entire aircraft carrier."

"What does the ONI and Army Intel have so far?" Manning asked.

"Approximately eight hours before Colonel Merrill was assassinated in Tokyo, another S-1 intel officer attached with the U.S. Embassy in Japan was reported AWOL," Brognola replied. "Captain Gerald Kenshaw was one of the few people who knew about Merrill's top-secret assignment. Kenshaw is *still* listed as missing from the morning report."

"So he gave the enemy the information," Yakov mused.

"But did he defect and give the information willingly," Manning added, "or did the terrorists force him to talk?"

"A psychological profile on Kenshaw seems to rule out the former," Brognola said. "The man's record as a professional career soldier was exceptional, and his superiors vouch for his loyalty."

"British Intelligence felt the same way about George Blake," McCarter commented as he drank from a can of Coca-Cola. "And he turned out to be a bloody Russian spy."

"Anything is possible," Yakov allowed. "But why would a double agent blow his cover just to have a cryptographer killed?"

"And Kenshaw didn't know about the conference scheduled to be held on the *Undefeated*," Brognola added. "That operation was handled by the ONI. However, a Lieutenant Commander John Barsa knew the locale where the aircraft carrier was to receive Admiral Samuels's helicopter."

"Has Barsa vanished as well?" Manning asked.

"That's right," Brognola confirmed. "He was listed as missing from the morning report the same day the attack on the admiral's chopper occurred."

"If terrorists kidnapped Barsa," Rafael remarked, "that means they managed to break him and forced him to talk in less than twenty-four hours."

"That's why the president considers this matter so critical," Brognola stated. "Both Kenshaw and Barsa had been trained to resist interrogation tactics. They had received advance instruction in such methods as hypnotic suggestion, psychological stress and physical torture."

"I was a prisoner in Castro's El Principe," Rafael

declared, referring to Cuba's infamous political prison. "Believe me, *any* man—no matter how tough or well trained he might be—can be broken."

"That's right," the Fed agreed. "If the interrogators have enough time. But everything suggests that Barsa or Kenshaw couldn't have been broken under torture—not in less than twenty-four hours."

"No man can be certain of that until he's endured such torment himself," the Cuban insisted.

"What about drugs?" Yakov inquired. "Scopolamine?"

"Barsa and Kenshaw both underwent extensive hypnosis to counteract scopolamine and other truth serums," Brognola answered. "When the needle is inserted, it serves as a key to trigger a posthypnotic state. The subject then relays false information previously fed into his subconscious."

"What about the GB/Sarin compound?" Manning asked. "The Red Anvil terrorists used it effectively enough on American military personnel when they tried to steal those Dessler Laser rifles for Libya. GB/Sarin turned GIs into robots who were unable to disobey any command. The Red Anvil bastards even ordered soldiers to shoot each other—and they did it!"

"None of us are bloody likely to forget that one," McCarter muttered.

"Fortunately," Brognola began, "because you were able to give us a vial of GB/Sarin, our scientists have been able to analyze the drug. Not only did they find a way to duplicate the compound, they also perfected an antiserum that can be taken as an immunization shot. The superdrug might have worked on Kenshaw, but Barsa had been vaccinated against the effects of GB/Sarin.''

"Jesus," McCarter said as he rose from his chair. "If the bastards didn't use threats, torture or drugs—how the hell did they get their victims to talk?''

And Rafael added, "Who are they? Is a terrorist outfit involved or is this a Soviet plot?''

"Perhaps both," Yakov commented. "The KGB was behind that business with the Japanese terrorists, Tigers of Justice, and they've been supplying training and arms and influencing the Japanese Red Army from day one.''

"According to my sources," Manning began, "the JRA ranks have been whittled down to less than a hundred members scattered all over the world. They're supposed to be in the Middle East, Africa, South America—just about everywhere *except* Japan.''

"The Japanese authorities certainly made things hot for the JRA," Rafael added. "And the terrorists never got very far looking for support from the public. That's why they ran off to join forces with other terrorist outfits with similar warped goals.''

"Don't dismiss the JRA," McCarter warned as he paced the office floor. The Briton was always a bundle of nervous energy, unable to sit still for long. "They might be scattered all over the bloody map, but that doesn't mean they can't make a nasty comeback. Everybody thought the Baader-Meinhof gang and the Weatherman were defunct until they both started raising hell again in 1981.''

"No one doubts that the JRA is still around," Manning assured him. "The question is: who among their ranks could mastermind such an operation? Takashi and Shigenobu are dead, and Okamoto Kozo is in an Israeli prison.''

"There's still at least one potential leader left from the old guard," Yakov declared. "Tanaga Zeko.''

"Tanaga?" McCarter blinked with surprise. "Wasn't he identified as the advance man for the Lod Airport massacre in Israel?''

Brognola smiled, but Yakov nodded. "Twenty-six people were killed and seventy-two wounded. Tanaga helped set up that bloodbath. He still has to answer for that.''

"You'll have to dig him up first," McCarter commented. "Tanaga was reportedly killed by a land mine in a terrorist training camp in South Yemen.''

"The hell he was," Yakov replied gruffly. "Last year Mossad confirmed that was a cover story. Tanaga isn't dead.''

"Yes, he is, Yakov." Brognola finally spoke up. "That was recently *confirmed* by Colonel Phoenix himself.''

"Oh?" Yakov smiled. "My compliments to the colonel.''

"Well, amigos," Rafael sighed, "we aren't going

to take care of anything by sitting around talking about it.''

"Bloody right,'' McCarter agreed eagerly. "Let's get our arses to Japan and find the bastards so we can rehabilitate them by blowing their heads off.''

"Yeah,'' Manning said. "Keio can join the party when we get there.''

Manning referred to Phoenix Force's absent member, Keio Ohara. Rather than order the young Japanese to fly from Tokyo to attend a briefing on a mission to Japan, Brognola had already contacted Keio and told him to await the arrival of his partners.

"Has Kompei been contacted about this matter?'' Yakov asked, referring to the Japanese version of the CIA.

"Officially the Japanese don't know a damn thing about Phoenix Force,'' the Fed answered. "Unofficially, you'll be briefed by Colonel Ikeda Ken, a security officer for Kompei, when you arrive.''

"Ikeda?'' Manning frowned. "I thought it was Nakada who was in charge of Japanese internal security.''

"He...recently retired,'' Brognola explained.

"Colonel Phoenix confirmed that, too, eh?'' Rafael laughed.

Brognola shrugged. He seldom relayed any more confidential material to personnel than was required. Of course, Phoenix Force was composed of top-notch pros who worked best when they were told everything up front. The Force really had only one superior—Colonel John Phoenix.

The Fed knew that although McCarter, Encizo, Manning, Ohara and Katzenelenbogen were not born in the United States—Rafael being the only naturalized U.S. citizen of the lot—they were all-American in spirit. Five warriors who loved freedom, hated injustice and would charge into Hell to fight for what they believed.

"What about weaponry?" McCarter inquired. "Japan has even more idiot restrictions on firearms than England."

"May I make a suggestion?" Manning said. "One of my company's associate organizations, North America International, has a branch office in Tokyo. We can disassemble some weapons and put the parts in with machine equipment inside a couple of crates."

"It'll pass through X-rays," Rafael agreed. "But North America International doesn't ship machinery."

"You know that and I know that," the Canadian said, grinning. "But do the Japanese customs people know it?"

"We'll probably be restricted to close-quarters weapons," Yakov mused. "But at least we can transport our personal side arms that way—as well as a machine pistol or two."

"Yeah," Rafael nodded. "And I'm sure Keio has some goodies tucked away we can borrow while we're in town."

"We can probably get everything ready in about four hours," McCarter commented, glancing at the black face of his Le Gran wristwatch.

"Okay," Brognola said, "but I don't have to warn any of you about the craziness of Japanese terrorists. The Red Army has never been known to kill a hostage. And, if cornered, they'll resort to suicide tactics that would scare the hell out of a kamikaze pilot. You guys already encountered that sort of conduct when you went up against the Tigers of Justice."

"Those lunatics were modern-day *ninja*," Manning commented. "Not likely there are many more of their kind still around."

"Don't bet on it," Brognola replied dryly, knowing Colonel Phoenix had recently returned from an incredible adventure in Japan. Bolan had encountered a plot that involved a clan of Japanese Yakuza gangsters and a number of *ninja* espionage agents, trained in the manner of their ancient forerunners and specializing in assassination.

"We never take our job lightly," Rafael assured him. "Except for McCarter here. When that happens, we just get him drunk and put him to bed so he doesn't get in our way."

"At least I don't drink liquor with a worm at the bottom of the bottle," McCarter responded.

"If you've nothing else for us," Yakov said to Brognola, "we'd best be on our way to Japan."

The Fed nodded. The members of Phoenix Force were cut from the same Viking cloth as the Executioner himself. Bolan understood his fellow warriors. "Just tell them the problem," he had said, "then turn them loose."

"You guys know as much about this business as I

do,'' Brognola told them. "This is *big*. The national security of the United States, Japan and possibly the entire free world may well depend on the success or failure of your mission.''

Brognola did not add that what really worried him was that Phoenix Force might already be too late....

3

The Boeing 747 was registered as property of North America International, which rented facilities at Dulles International Airport. Most of the plane's passengers were business people with the corporation or related associations that also had branches in Japan.

The four members of Phoenix Force were the only passengers seated in the first-class section. Gary Manning had told the head stewardess that he and his colleagues had a considerable amount of confidential business to discuss, and he asked that they not be disturbed. Although assured of privacy, the four men still conversed quietly, aware that security can never be exaggerated during a mission.

"We should have asked Brognola to get us a military jet," David McCarter commented. "I could fly the rig, and we'd be in Tokyo in five hours."

"Yes," Yakov agreed. "But we'd have to land a fighter jet at a military base. Probably an American installation. The security leaks have all occurred among the U.S. Armed Forces, so we'd be taking too great a risk that way."

"Yeah," Rafael sighed. "But at least we'd have

been able to get our weapons on a Douglas EB-66 without having to lock them in crates and transport them in a cargo hold.''

"The only person who could get a weapon aboard is you, Yakov," McCarter added.

"Everything," the Israeli said, smiling, "has certain advantages—even an artificial arm."

Katzenelenbogen wore a prosthetic device attached to the stump of his right arm. The "hand" was made of steel and insulated wires and cables, with four fingers and a thumb. Although it appeared quite lifelike when clad in a pearl gray glove, the contraption was not as practical or versatile as the three-prong hook Yakov favored. However, the "hand" attracted less attention and made the middle-aged Israeli inconspicuous in a crowd.

In addition to serving a cosmetic purpose, the artificial hand had another unique feature. The steel index finger was hollow; it was the barrel of a built-in pistol. A single-shot device, it fired a .22 Magnum cartridge, detonated by a 9-volt battery that could be activated by manipulation of muscles in the stump of Yakov's arm. There was a safety catch located at the "palm" to prevent firing the weapon by accident.

"Not all of us have an excuse for carrying two and a half pounds of metal on an airplane," Rafael commented as he unbuttoned his shirt at the throat. "But there's more than one way to get a weapon through security."

He reached inside his shirt and removed a leather

thong from his neck. The cord had been strung through the eyelet of a small black object, shaped like a dirk.

"What the hell is that?" Manning inquired. "It looks like a plastic knife."

"It's an A.G. Russell 'CIA letter opener,'" Rafael explained. "And it's made of fiberglass and nylon, but tough as metal. It's designed similar to the A.G. Russell 'Sting' boot knife. See how thick the blade is? It isn't very sharp, but the construction reinforces the point and makes it ideal for thrust attacks at close quarters."

"Impressive," McCarter said, smiling. "If we get attacked by any envelopes, you're ready for them."

"What do you guys make of this mission?" Manning asked as he sipped black coffee and leafed through a Japanese phrase book.

"My guess is that the terrorists are squeezing information out of their victims through torture," the Cuban responded. "It's crude, ruthless and effective. Terrorists favor such methods."

"Drugs are faster," Katz stated.

"But not as reliable," Encizo insisted. "Scopolamine can be beaten by posthypnosis, and it can't be given in excess because a large dose can be fatal. Besides, scopolamine isn't generally part of a terrorist's training. Even professional terrorists are more apt to use torture. I've been through it, my friends. I know about torture."

"So do I," the Israeli reminded him. "And we both know it takes time in order to be reliable. If a torturer rushes and causes too much pain too quickly, he'll throw a victim into shock or kill him outright.''

"We'll learn how they did it when we find the bastards," McCarter said, shrugging his shoulders. "This mission is the same as always—search and destroy."

"I just hope we don't have to search very long," Encizo added.

"I'll drink to that," the Briton replied with a grin, and raised his can of Coca-Cola to salute the Cuban.

"You'd drink to a rattlesnake's birthday," Encizo said, laughing.

"Bloody right," McCarter admitted. "I've got nothing against reptiles regardless of race, creed or national origin. My only real prejudice is against goddamn terrorists of any sort."

"And *I* can drink to that," the Cuban agreed.

"Are you two really all that bloodthirsty?" Manning inquired.

"Getting squeamish in your old age, Manning?" the Englishman chided.

"I'm a professional," the Canadian told him. "I've got a job to do, and that will prevent international terrorism from tearing down civilization throughout the free world. Since terrorists will resort to any sort of tactics to accomplish their goals, we have to deal with them in just as ruthless a manner more often than not."

"We're all in the same line of business, amigo," the Cuban remarked. "None of us feels any need to justify what we do. Frankly, I don't know why the hell you're trying to make excuses for something you know *has to be* done.''

"I don't enjoy killing people," Manning said. "Not even terrorists."

"Jesus," McCarter snorted. "None of us enjoys it, but I'll admit it doesn't bother me much to kill terrorists. And I generally feel a certain satisfaction when I rid the world of some human parasites. I'd rather kill murderous fanatics than stuff my hands in my bloody pockets and stand by while those bastards try to wreck the world for whatever lunatic cause they're supposedly fighting for."

"Gary," Katzenelenbogan began, "you've always known that we often have to kill terrorists to stop them. You've been doing this sort of thing too long to feel guilty about it. What's really bothering you?"

"Maybe I'm afraid of becoming as callous about life and death as the people we're fighting," the Canadian answered. "My life has always consisted of work and responsibilities. When my wife divorced me, she claimed I was a workaholic. I couldn't argue with her, either."

"So what if you are a workaholic?" the Cuban asked. "You always seemed sort of proud of it."

"But she also said that my work meant more to me than people did," Manning continued. "Of course she was talking about my job with the demolitions company and the security agency. That was before Phoenix Force was formed...."

"Screw your ex-wife," McCarter said bluntly.

Manning glared at the Briton.

"Gary," Katz said gently, "the fact that you can feel concern about your own humanity proves you're in no danger of losing it."

Manning nodded. It was both a reply and a silent thanks to the Israeli.

"Well I'm in danger of losing my bloody lunch," McCarter complained in mock anger. "Whoever is flying this plane must have been a donkey jockey. We'll have bruises on our backsides before we get to Japan."

"That's what I like about you, McCarter," Encizo remarked. "You always take hardships in stride."

KEIO OHARA steered his Toyota sports wagon into the main parking lot of Tokyo International Airport. He showed his security pass to a guard who studied the photo on the card and compared it with the face that peered at him from the car window. Keio was a young man, not yet thirty, with jet black hair, a handsome sleek face and dark almond-shaped eyes.

Although he was of pure Japanese descent, Keio was sometimes mistaken for a Eurasian because of his straight nose and his height. Even while he was seated behind the wheel of his Toyota, his height was obvious to the guard. The security cop also noted Keio's immaculate attire—a conservative black suit with a pale blue shirt and a maroon tie.

"Domo, Ohara-*san,"* said the guard, thanking Keio for his cooperation and bowing as he returned the pass.

"Do itashi-mah'teh," Keio replied.

He drove the sports wagon around a massive hangar and located the runway where Flight 912 from Washington, D.C., had just landed. Keio noticed a black limousine had already arrived, set to meet Phoenix Force and transport them to Kompei Headquarters. For additional security and to save time, the car was supposed to pick them up at the runway, allowing the visitors to avoid customs inside the airport terminal.

Odd, Keio thought. He had spoken with Ikeda Ken and the chief of Kompei Special Internal Affairs had agreed to cancel the limo so Ohara could meet his friends at the airport instead.

Keio pulled up to the side of the hangar and parked his Toyota. Instinct warned him something might be wrong, yet he did not want to act in a rash manner in case his sixth sense had its wiring crossed.

Passengers began to deplane. Yakov, McCarter, Rafael and Manning were the first to walk down the ramp. Keio's apprehension increased as he watched the four men head toward the limousine. If something was wrong, Keio would have to act soon....

Then he saw the doors of the limo open and three men dressed in black suits emerge. Each had a raincoat draped over his forearm. Two more men were still inside the car. Four other figures, dressed in blue airport-maintenance coveralls, also approached from a cargo truck. Two carried canvas bags large enough to conceal machine pistols.

"Oh, hell," David McCarter muttered under his breath when he saw the three hard-faced Japanese at the limo. The trio aimed their raincoat-clad arms at Phoenix Force. The muzzles of silenced weapons jutted from under the cloth.

"Double hell, amigo," Rafael added as he glanced over his shoulder at the four "maintenance men" who had opened their bags and were reaching inside for weapons.

"If they hit us in the airport, they'll pay hell trying to get out of here," Manning commented.

"They'll want to take us to a more isolated area," Yakov agreed. "But don't think they won't open fire if we resist."

"Welcome to Nippon," one of the terrorists standing near the limo declared with a sly smile. "You come in our car. No come, we kill you."

"What weapons we have with us are only good at close quarters," Rafael quietly reminded his friends.

"Hell," McCarter groaned again. "There are too many of them to try to jump the bastards."

"We have to go along with them," Yakov stated. "Just pray they get careless."

Keio saw his four partners approach the limo. He opened a briefcase on the seat beside him and extracted a huge steel pistol with a thick eight-inch barrel. The .44 AutoMag was an awesome weapon. The most powerful autoloading handgun in the world, it could bring down a charging bull elephant with one shot.

Ohara gathered his AutoMag in his right hand, seized the steering wheel with his left and stomped on the gas pedal. The Toyota sports wagon roared as it lurched from the hangar and sped toward the limo.

A "maintenance man" pivoted, saw the vehicle racing forward and quickly yanked a Skorpion machine pistol from a canvas bag. A spray of 7.65mm slugs coughed from the Czech miniblaster's silenced barrel. The small-caliber bullets ricocheted off the shatterproof glass of Keio's specially equipped Toyota.

The Toyota charged into the "maintenance men." Screaming in fear and rage, the terrorists bolted in a desperate attempt to avoid Ohara's ruthless attack. Keio swung the Toyota's nose sharply and slammed into one of the fleeing gunmen, sending the man's body hurtling across the pavement in an awkward cartwheel. Keio swerved and rammed another terrorist. The impact propelled the killer five feet into the air. His broken body dropped onto the roof of the speeding Toyota, bounced off and fell to earth in a lifeless heap.

The other members of Phoenix Force had already taken advantage of the distraction. Yakov raised his right arm and pointed the gloved index finger at the face of the terrorist spokesman. Flame exploded from the end of the Israeli's fake finger and a .22 Magnum mercury-filled bullet tore into the killer's right eye. Blood erupted from the eye socket as the bullet sliced through his brain. The explosive round then struck the back of the man's skull and blew off almost half of the goon's head.

Gary Manning clubbed another terrorist across the forearm with the bottom of his left fist. The blow knocked the man's raincoat and a silencer-equipped Nambu 9mm pistol to the ground. Before the surprised terrorist could react, Manning drove a right uppercut to the man's solar plexus.

The piece of Japanese filth gasped as the wind was knocked out of his lungs, but he still tried to knee Manning in the groin and attempted a *shuto* slash with the side of his right hand. Moving with uncanny speed for a big man, the powerful Canadian dodged the knee lift and scooped up the terrorist's leg with his right forearm. Manning stepped forward, snaking one arm over his opponent's shoulder and the other between his legs.

The terrorist screamed as Manning suddenly picked him up and turned him upside down in a crotch lift. The Canadian quickly dashed his adversary against the hood of the limousine. The small of the man's back smashed into metal, and the vulnerable fifth lumbar vertebra shattered on impact. He rolled off the car hood and fell to the ground, his backbone broken.

Rafael Encizo took care of another member of the terrorist "welcome wagon." His left hand swept the killer's gun arm toward the ground while his right extracted the A.G. Russell "letter opener" from a jacket pocket. The gunman fired a muted 9mm round at the pavement. The bullet ricocheted and tore a vicious furrow in the terrorist's calf muscle.

The killer opened his mouth to scream, but Rafael struck before the sound could materialize. Sharp pointed nylon punched through the thin skin at the hollow of the terrorist's throat. Blood gushed from his mouth as the man hopelessly clawed at the black handle of the letter opener lodged deep inside his throat.

Rafael did not waste time watching the goon drown in his own blood. He quickly twisted the pistol from the dying man's grasp and threw himself to the pavement. The Cuban had not acted a moment too soon as a limo door opened and another terrorist emerged with a Soviet-made AK-47 assault rifle in his hands. Rafael rolled on his side and aimed the unfamiliar Nambu pistol at the gunman's head. The pistol uttered a choked snarl through its sound suppressor, and a 9mm slug burned a merciless hole under the gunman's jawbone. The bullet cut through the goon's tongue and pierced the roof of his mouth, finding a resting place in the terrorist's brain.

When his partners jumped the trio of killers dressed in undertaker's basic black, David McCarter turned his attention to the two remaining "maintenance men." Both had drawn Skorpion machine pistols and were firing at the Toyota. The terrorists' shots were poorly aimed because they were too busy trying to outrun the vehicle.

McCarter hurled his briefcase at one of the fleeing gunmen.

The sturdy luggage struck the legs of the running man and abruptly tripped him. The Japanese trooper of terror fell flat on his face, the Skorpion skidding away from his fingers. McCarter immediately dashed forward and leaped into the air. He came down, feet first, on the back of the fallen man's neck. The ruthless stomp crushed vertebrae.

McCarter then dived to the ground and grabbed the dead man's discarded machine pistol. He rose to one knee and trained the Czech-made chatterbox on the other terrorist who was still playing tag with Keio's Toyota. McCarter squeezed the trigger, and a three-round burst of 7.65mm projectiles hissed from the silenced Skorpion to rip a trio of gory holes in the center of the terrorist's chest. The gunman's body buckled, and he staggered before he slumped to the ground.

Keio saw one of the doors open on the side of the limo opposite Phoenix Force. He turned the steering wheel savagely to swing his Toyota past the nose of the big black car. The last member of the terrorist hit team had emerged from the limo, clutching a Makarov pistol. He spotted Keio's vehicle and opened fire, crouched behind the open car door for cover.

Keio's Toyota came to a stop as a 9mm round buried itself in the metal skin on the passenger's side of the wagon. The body of the sports wagon was only lightly armored to avoid making it too heavy for adequate speed. Keio jumped out of the car at the driver's side. He knelt behind the Toyota and used the hood for a benchrest, both hands fisted around the big AutoMag.

Few men have the necessary strength in their fingers and wrists to handle such a powerful handgun. The recoil is formidable in a weapon that packs enough punch to send a Cape buffalo to Boot Hill. Mack Bolan was such a man and so was Keio Ohara.

The steel cannon bellowed, and a long tongue of orange flame burst from its muzzle. Keio's arms rose with the recoil, climbing smoothly above his head. The big .44-caliber slug struck the door of the limo and knifed through metal as though it were rice paper. The bullet penetrated the door and tore into the terrorist's belly. It severed his abdominal aorta and sizzled through his liver before it blasted an exit hole at his back the size of a silver dollar. One more insult to his Japanese ancestors crumbled to the ground—dead.

"You guys need a ride?" Ohara called to his teammates.

"This sort of thing won't improve the Japanese tourist trade," McCarter growled as he tossed the Skorpion aside and scooped up a discarded Nambu pistol.

"Save it for your memoirs, David," Rafael said gruffly, relieving another dead terrorist of a Makarov. "We've got to get out of here before every cop in Tokyo shows up."

"Too bad we couldn't have taken one or two of the bastards alive," Manning commented as he jogged to the Toyota.

"Hell," McCarter snorted. "We were lucky to keep ourselves alive."

"And staying that way might not be easy," Yakov added, joining the others as they climbed into Keio's car.

4

Ikeda Ken sighed as he poured green *cha* into small porcelain cups. "Such violence occurred this day," he said sadly. "It is most regrettable."

Ikeda's guests were the five men of Phoenix Force who had assembled in a small office in a communications building on Niju Street in Tokyo. The quaint little office, with plastic furniture, a green carpet and bamboo window blinds, was rented to Kompei under a cover name and served as a safehouse for Japanese Intel operations.

"Those terrorists were set up for us," David McCarter declared bluntly. "They knew about the limousine, and they knew every detail about the rendezvous Kompei had arranged for us. That's a bit more than 'regrettable.'"

"So we've both got a problem, Mr. Ikeda," Rafael added. "Your organization has a security leak and we've been burned."

Ikeda frowned. "Burned? I'm sorry. I don't understand."

"It means our cover story is ruined," Yakov explained. "Our enemies have identified us, and our mission here is no longer a secret."

"Ah, I understand now." Ikeda nodded. A small, slightly built man with a round face and horn-rimmed glasses, he looked more like an accountant than the chief of Kompei's Internal Intelligence. "Tea, gentlemen?"

"*Domo arigato,* Ikeda-*san*," Gary Manning said as their host placed the tea tray on a Plexiglas table. When thanking him, Gary had addressed Ikeda as "Ikeda-sir," the most courteous form of address.

The Kompei man bowed in reply, appreciating the Canadian's manners. Manning had dealt with Japanese businessmen in the past, and he realized how important etiquette is in their culture. The Japanese are a polite dignified people.

The Japanese place great value on *enryo*, a personal code of conduct that emphasizes constraint and reserve. Yet they are an emotional people, moved by simple poetry and subtle colors. They tend to be passionately devoted to their jobs, political beliefs and, most of all, their families.

Traditionally they are an explosive and energetic breed—a part of their nature that is evident in the movies and television programs they favor. But they have a remarkably low crime rate for a country that is so densely populated. This has nothing to do with Japan's restrictions on firearms or other weapons, because gangsters and terrorists disregard such laws in the Orient just as they do everywhere else. Japan simply has fewer criminals and even the Yakuza gangs tend to act with restraint to a degree. Unlawful behavior is dishonorable and an insult to one's family, which is all-important in Japan.

In 1972 a nest of the major leaders of the JRA was located in an abandoned building in Karvizawa. Police bombarded the terrorist headquarters with tear gas and powerful jets of ice-cold water before storming the building, armed to the teeth and ready for battle. The public applauded the siege. It was a vivid example of how Japan refuses to tolerate terrorism. After all, such conduct is not *enryo*.

"I share your concern, my friends," Ikeda assured his guests as he sat in a curved-back chair. "But I believe the situation is not quite as grim as it appears."

"The limousine had been sent by Kompei, correct?" Yakov inquired, sipping his tea.

"The arrangements had been made, yes," Ikeda confessed. "But I am certain Ohara-*san* has explained that he was to meet you at the airport instead."

"Bloody lucky for us he did," McCarter commented as he fired a cigarette.

"Indeed," Ikeda said, nodding. "The limousine was to be canceled. However, the agent assigned to serve as driver was abducted sometime yesterday. Clearly this is an act by the same villains responsible for the terrorist actions directed against American Intelligence that you have come to investigate."

"We didn't come to investigate," Rafael stated. "We came to stop the bastards—permanently."

"I was informed as to the methods you gentlemen

favor," Ikeda announced, smiling. "Officially, my government uses violence only as a last resort. Unofficially, we will do *anything* to prevent a revival of the destructive activities of terrorism. In the late sixties the Japanese Red Army had almost four hundred members. They were responsible for numerous armed robberies, violent street riots and the murder of many police officers. This *must not* be allowed to happen again."

"Excuse me, Ikeda-*san*," Keio said softly. "You say our situation is not as grave as it appears, yet the terrorists abducted your agent and obviously extracted classified information from him...."

"But that information was most limited," Ikeda replied. "The man was simply ordered to meet four Americans arriving on Flight 912 and transport them to Kompei headquarters. We had no descriptions of any of you. In fact, you all seem more like Europeans than Americans. Since you terminated the only terrorists who could have identified you and Ohara-*san* brought you here instead of Kompei headquarters, you have not been 'burned' at all."

"Perhaps not," Yakov said, "but there may have been an observation team watching the airport from a distance to report its success or failure. That doesn't really make any difference now. We still have a job to do. If the terrorists come out from under their rocks to try to kill us, they'll save us the trouble of finding them first."

"A dangerous tactic, Katzen...ah..." Ikeda began, fumbling on Yakov's name.

"Just call me Yakov or Katz," the Israeli put in with a smile. "And there is *no* safe way to deal with terrorists, my friend."

"You realize you will be acting alone," the Kompei chief warned. "We can supply information and assist in certain matters—such as convincing the police that Kompei will take care of the incident at the airport. However, we cannot be actively involved in any commando operations you may choose to conduct."

"That suits us fine," Manning assured him. "Can you add any new information to what we already know about the terrorists?"

"*Hai*—yes," Ikeda replied, nodding. "A letter was sent to the prime minister's office. His staff sent it to us. The letter was apparently sent by the Red Cell."

"Red Cell?" McCarter frowned. "Sounds like a plasma center. I've heard of the Revolutionary Cells in West Germany, but I didn't think they'd ever gotten involved in any operations outside of Europe."

"I regret to admit that the Red Cell is entirely Japanese," Ikeda sighed. "It seems to consist of former members of the old JRA who have joined forces with militant isolationists. In the letter they made several outrageous demands."

"Such as?" Yakov inquired.

"They want all United States military personnel expelled from all Japanese properties, including Okinawa," the Kompei chief explained. "The Red Cell also demands that Japan end all export to

America and Western Europe and increase trade with the 'progressive' societies of the Soviet Union, North Korea and other Communist and pro-Marxist countries.''

"Stupid bastards," McCarter muttered. "If their idiot demands were met, they'd turn Japan into a satellite country under control of the USSR.''

"If the JRC is similar to the Japanese Red Army," Keio remarked, "they'll be willing to negotiate terms for more than most terrorist outfits, but they won't back down unless they get at least part of what they want.''

"Small comfort," Manning commented. "*All* of their demands are absurd and nonnegotiable.''

"The Red Cell must think their secret for extracting information from subjects is important enough to frighten us into agreeing to anything," Ikeda said.

"They couldn't have anything that could threaten the security of the free world more effectively," Yakov stated.

"And what's worse is the JRC might sell information to the Soviets, the Chinese, Khaddafi, anyone else they want," Rafael said.

"Or they can pass on the secret to the process itself," Manning stated grimly. "God help us if they already have.''

The telephone on Ikeda's desk rang. The Kompei man answered it. Only Keio understood the rapid Japanese Ikeda spoke into the phone—although the intel officer listened more than he talked.

"The Tokyo police delivered some vital information to my department that may be of use to us all,'' Ikeda declared. ''The dead men at the airport carried forged identification, but a computer check on their fingerprints has identified four of them as members of the Japanese Red Army still wanted for various crimes. They had fled the country more than ten years ago. Autopsies tell us they've undergone plastic surgery to alter their faces.''

''Well,'' Manning said, unimpressed by the news, ''that just proves the JRC is a highly professional terrorist outfit—something we already knew.''

''Ah,'' Ikeda said, smiling, ''but there is more. Three of the dead men had business cards from the Hoshiro Fish Company, located on the harbor at Iwaki.''

''Business cards don't necessarily prove a connection,'' Rafael mused. ''But if all three men were actually employed at this fish company. . . .''

''My people at Kompei headquarters are looking into that,'' Ikeda assured him. ''Also, five of the terrorists had membership cards to the Zembu Dojo, a martial-arts school here in Tokyo.''

''Sounds like we have a couple leads to check out,'' Rafael stated.

''We also have to get our crates, which are still at the airport,'' Manning reminded the others. ''All our equipment is in them.''

''Right,'' McCarter agreed. ''But we'd better not waste any time. I think we should check out the martial-arts school pretty damn quick. If the terrorists are associated with it, they'll soon abandon the place and head underground.''

"Might check out the harbor operation, too,'' the Cuban suggested.

"So we have our work cut out for us,'' Yakov commented. "And we'd better get some results fast. I have a feeling we don't have very much time.''

5

"This is too much," Professor Ouzu Yoichi insisted as he marched across the yellow tile floor of the massive control center.

The "war room" of the Japanese Red Cell was filled with computers, international communications radios and other equipment. It was a sophisticated tribute to the technology of twentieth-century evil.

Yoichi suited his surroundings, his painfully thin body clad in a white smock two sizes too large. His gaunt face was highlighted by hollow cheeks and large round glasses that grotesquely magnified his eyes.

"Too much?" Professor Edward Oshimi raised his shaggy gray eyebrows. "You have always known our ultimate goals, Ouzu. You always seemed to believe in them as much as I."

Although Oshimi was a year older than Yoichi, he appeared at least five years younger. A stocky heavy-set man, Oshimi still moved with the step of a young man. He shaved his head, creating a sinister bullet-like appearance, and usually wore a traditional *yukata* robe. Oshimi's dark eyes flashed when he glared at Yoichi as if demanding proof of his loyalty.

"Of course, I believe in our cause, Edo," Yoichi assured him, addressing Oshimi by the nickname he favored over his first name. Edo was the old name of the city now known as Tokyo. "But you're trying to accomplish too much too fast."

"We must move quickly, Ouzu," Oshimi insisted. "My sources inform me that a great opportunity is about to present itself to us like a gift from the gods."

"If we continue to act rashly, we're bound to encourage the authorities to concentrate on searching for us," Yoichi said. "If they find us. . . ."

"They won't," Oshimi declared. "And this is no time for us to retreat."

He stabbed a finger onto a button of a control panel. Yellow, green and red lights immediately appeared on the face of a large map of the world that covered one wall. The east coast of Japan was dotted with multicolored bulbs from Hamanatsu to Sendai. Red lights marked Tokyo and the Trench of Japan. Okinawa and the Hawaiian Islands were also sprinkled with lights, but none of these was crimson.

"Need I remind you what we've already accomplished?" Oshimi demanded as he thrust his forefinger at the map. "The yellow lights represent the strategic locations of our followers—the Japanese Red Cell under command of Daito-*san*. The green lights are future target sites, and the red signify successful assaults on the enemy."

"What color lights will represent failure?" Yoichi inquired dryly.

Oshimi stiffened with anger. Yoichi did not look away from the other man's furious expression. He realized Edo was a ruthless fanatic. But Yoichi was an indispensable part of the plans to build a new empire, too. Both men were devoted to a common goal of ultimate conquest.

Oshimi wanted to be a twentieth-century shogun, an all-powerful military dictator commanding the New Empire of Japan. However, Yoichi, a dedicated Communist, dreamed of becoming the Lenin of Nippon. Like most zealots, Yoichi could recognize fanaticism in others, yet failed to acknowledge it in himself.

"The incident at Tokyo airport was a fluke," Oshimi declared. "Daito-*san* isn't certain what went wrong, but it is a minor problem. How much trouble can four Americans cause?"

"Daito knew they were experts," Yoichi said. "He sent nine of his best soldiers to apprehend them—or kill them if they resisted. Nine men, Edo."

"We have dozens more to replace them," Oshimi replied. "Casualties must be expected in war. No worthy conquest comes easily, my friend."

"I appreciate that," Yoichi assured him. "But Japan has always been able to deal with terrorism quite well on its own. Whoever these Americans are, they must be very special for the *Nihon-no* government to send for them...."

"We are not terrorists," Oshimi snapped. "We are fighting to reclaim the glory of Japan."

"It is said Yamazaki Hideo attempted this same goal," Yoichi remarked.

"Yamazaki was a fool," Oshimi answered. "He thought he could use killer bacteria in a direct attack on the United States. Someone found out about his scheme and stopped him."

Neither man knew that "someone" had been Mack Bolan.

"Yamazaki was insane," Oshimi continued. "He wanted to turn back the clock to the twelfth century. The lunatic considered himself to be an ancient *daimyo* warlord. His estate was guarded by men armed with samurai swords instead of guns. The madman even hired *ninja* warriors to carry out assassination missions.

"Our plans are totally different," Oshimi insisted. "We aren't attempting an absurd assault on the United States. That damn country is too large and technologically advanced for such tactics to be successful. We are not trying to ignore the twentieth century. No. We will simply bring Japan out of the shadow of the Western powers to claim its rightful place as a strong independent country—an empire with sovereignty over other lands and well-armed military bases scattered throughout the world."

Yoichi was finding Oshimi's lecture tiresome. "You forget the Americans...."

"I *never* forget the Americans," the other man snapped. "I never forget that I was born in that accursed nation. Americans claim they believe in justice, freedom and equality. Damn their lies. My family was sent to a concentration camp in Oregon during World War II. Why? Because they were Japanese. Oh, they were American citizens, but the color of their skin and the shape of their eyes made them the enemy to the tyrants in Washington.

"After the war this prejudice against Orientals continued," Oshimi said bitterly. "America didn't go to war against Russia when it took Eastern Europe by force, yet they responded differently in Korea and Vietnam. Why? Because the white ruling class feared an Oriental world power. America claims to be a friend to Japan, yet our people are still oppressed by the Westerners. When I was young, they scoffed at merchandise 'made in Japan.' Now the Americans are angry because Japanese automobiles, watches and television sets are less expensive and better quality than their own products.

"Instead of admitting that American workers are greedy and lazy and lack pride in their work, they want to restrict Japanese imports. I know Americans all too well, Ouzu."

Of course you do, Yoichi thought. *You are an American.* But he said, "The Americans that concern me are the four who arrived in Tokyo today."

"Why do you worry about this slight matter?" Oshimi demanded. "Kompei and the police have been unable to stop us. Do you think four foreigners will be more successful?"

"They've been successful enough so far," Yoichi reminded him. "Nine of our men...."

"We will not delay our plans simply because one

small squad of our soldiers was killed," Oshimi insisted. "Daito-*san* will take care of the American mercenaries if they cause any more trouble. Nothing can stop us, Ouzu. Japan will soon be a great empire, feared and respected throughout the world. And the powers of the West will be brought to their knees, begging us for mercy."

A young Japanese terrorist entered the war room. The Red Cell follower was dressed in a khaki uniform with a Sam Browne gun belt strapped around his lean waist. He approached the scientists and bowed. Oshimi returned the gesture, Yoichi did not bother. Unlike Oshimi, Yoichi cared little for Japanese customs and traditions. The hard-line Communist regarded such things as remnants of Japan's former imperialistic past, but he humored Oshimi's fondness for "silly meaningless gestures designed to repress the masses."

"Comrade Hatsumi wishes to know what you want done with the prisoner," the JRC trooper explained. "He says that the Kompei agent has probably been milked dry of any information that would be of use to us. Comrade Hatsumi suggests termination of the swine."

"By all means, Comrade Ishizuka," Oshimi replied. "The Kompei man is of no further use to us now."

"He wasn't of much use from the beginning," Yoichi commented. "Lieutenant Demura is just a minor officer in Kompei. Hardly worth the effort to abduct him."

"We'll discuss this later, professor," Oshimi said sharply. "Comrade Ishizuka, please instruct Hatsumi to terminate the prisoner."

"Hai, Oshimi-sama," the JRC soldier said, bowing.

Oshimi waited until Ishizuka left the room, then turned to Yoichi. "You know better than to talk that way in front of one of the men," he snapped.

"That was careless," Yoichi admitted. "But so was bringing Demura here. The only reason we seized the man was that he was supposed to be the driver of the car Kompei was to send to the airport to meet the Americans. He should have been terminated in Japan before we moved the equipment here. In fact it would have been better if we hadn't abducted him at all, considering what happened."

"I'm weary of hearing about those troublesome Americans," Oshimi sighed.

"And I'm tired of arguing with you about dangerous and unnecessary risks to our operation," Yoichi replied bluntly. "Bringing Demura here was such a risk."

"A moot point," Oshimi said with a shrug, "since he is to be dealt with now."

LIEUTENANT DEMURA had fully regained consciousness, but he allowed his body to hang limply as a pair of JRC storm troopers dragged him from the Room of Madness. Demura did not know what his captors called the place, but he had christened it the Room of

Madness because when he was inside it he found himself questioning his sanity.

The room was bizarre. It resembled the control center of the ridiculous villains in the *Godzilla* movies Demura had seen as a boy at Saturday matinees in Kyoto. The absurd films featured alien enemies from another planet who planned to take over the world with various giant monsters, and only Godzilla, a huge fire-breathing reptile, could save planet Earth. Even as a boy, Demura had wondered why Japan, which had produced such classics as *The Seven Samurai*, continued to make movies with an overgrown lizard for a hero.

But the Room of Madness was real and so were the villains. They were not aliens from a distant galaxy, and Godzilla was not going to rescue mankind from the Japanese Red Cell. The hokey movies were science fiction and no extraterrestrials of fantasy could be as frightening as the reality of terrorist fanatics with a fearsome technology at their command.

Demura was not certain who his captors were or why they had seized him. He was not even certain if he had answered any of their questions in the Room of Madness. Demura had been only semiconscious most of the time since his capture because of the sedatives that were injected into his veins every four hours.

However, his keepers had failed to follow the schedule closely enough, and the sedatives had worn off.

Demura was fully awake as the terrorists hauled him into a corridor.

Yet what could he do? Unarmed and outnumbered, without any idea where he was being held or why, Demura was uncertain what action to take. Still he could not allow himself to be drugged into submission again. He had to do something. . . .

Another JRC terrorist marched toward the trio. Like the two men who held Demura's arms, the third storm trooper also wore a paramilitary uniform— bush shirt and khaki slacks with a holstered side arm on his hip.

"What are you two doing with the prisoner?" Ishizuka demanded as he approached.

"We are taking him back to his cell, comrade," one of the guards replied.

"No need for that," Ishizuka told them. "He is to be terminated."

"Shoot him?" one of the sadistic guards asked eagerly.

"Gunshots are noisy," Ishizuka stated. "An injection of poison is silent and just as effective. Take him back to Comrade Hatsumi. . . ."

Demura realized he had nothing to lose by fighting his captors. With a *kiai* karate shout, Demura suddenly lashed a high roundhouse kick at the thug who held his left arm. His foot crashed into the startled JRC goon's face, breaking his upper and lower jaw on impact.

The guard was unconscious before he slumped to the floor. Demura swung his free arm to deliver a heel-of-the-palm blow to the other guard's face, smashing the guard's nose with the powerful blow. The sentry groaned and released Demura's right arm. The Kompei agent promptly rammed an elbow into the terrorist's solar plexus.

Ishizuka dragged a .357 Magnum from the holster on his hip. Demura quickly seized the stunned guard and hurled him into Ishizuka. The Magnum roared, drilling a 158-grain wadcutter through the terrorist's chest, blasting an exit hole as big as a half-dollar out of the man's back.

Demura lunged and karate chopped the revolver out of Ishizuka's hand. The terrorist reacted instantly and delivered a sideway *shuto* stroke of his own, slamming the edge of his hand into Demura's chest.

The Kompei agent stumbled backward into a wall, and Ishizuka swung a roundhouse kick at his opponent. Demura dodged the kick, but Ishizuka was well-trained in martial arts. When his foot struck the wall, he instantly turned his leg to punt a side kick into Demura's face.

Fortunately for Demura, most of the power of the kick had been spent on the wall and Ishizuka's follow-up lacked force. Nonetheless, the kick staggered Demura. He tasted blood and the corridor seemed to whirl before his eyes. He saw Ishizuka's form lurch forward for another attack.

His fingers arched like talons, the terrorist swung a vicious "tiger claw" stroke at Demura's eyes. The Kompei man blocked the attack with a forearm and rammed a *seiken* punch into Ishizuka's midsection.

The terrorist stumbled backward. Demura pressed his advantage and drove a fist into the point of his opponent's jaw.

Ishizuka struck out blindly, aiming stiffened fingers at Demura's throat. The Kompei agent parried the thrust with an elbow and quickly unleashed a diagonal *shuto* that struck Ishizuka full in the mouth. The terrorist's teeth caved in from the blow. Demura followed up with another karate chop to Ishizuka's left temple. A massive concussion ripped through the terrorist's brain, and he crumpled at his adversary's feet.

Even as Ishizuka fell, two more JRC soldiers appeared in the corridor. The guards had drawn their Magnums and swung the muzzles toward Demura. The Kompei man threw himself to the floor as the revolvers boomed.

Bullets hissed inches from Demura's hurtling form as he dived for Ishizuka's discarded weapon. His heart racing, his guts twisting, Demura hit the floor and seized the Combat Magnum. He rolled on his shoulder, landed on one knee and quickly opened fire at the uniformed terrorist troopers.

The big .357 thundered in his fist, kicking his arm high. Kompei training had included little combat shooting practice, and Demura was not used to the recoil of a big Magnum handgun. His first shot went too high and struck one of the JRC thugs in the left shoulder. Blood spurted from the wound as the impact spun the terrorist around in time to receive another .357 round under the right shoulder blade.

The mortally wounded guard fell as his partner scrambled for cover. The terrorists did not appear to be any better marksmen than Demura, and they lacked his courage and professionally honed reflexes. The Kompei man held the Magnum in both hands and fired once more. The bullet smashed into the wall as the surviving guard ducked around the corner.

Ammunition, Demura thought, aware that the Magnum held only one or two more cartridges in its cylinder. Crouched low with the .357 aimed at the enemy gunman's position, Demura reached for the shells slotted in the Sam Browne belt of one of the fallen guards.

The Kompei agent realized more terrorists would soon swoop down on him. Demura knew he could not kill them all, but he had joined Kompei to combat the enemies of his country. Lieutenant Demura almost welcomed an opportunity to die fighting for Japan and for a cause he believed in.

The ringing inside Demura's ears, caused by the loud reports of the Magnum in an enclosed area, deafened him to the threat that emerged from the Room of Madness. His back was turned to the figure clad in a white lab smock, who clenched a hypodermic syringe in his fist.

Hatsumi, the JRC technician and an assistant to Professor Yoichi, tried to swallow his fear as he crept up behind Demura. Hatsumi was not a fighting man. Thanks to warped idealistic notions encouraged by Marxist college professors, Hatsumi had altered his goals in life from medical science to international terrorism. He hated anything that upset the order of his life. Hatsumi was not supposed to get personally involved in violence. The rank and file of the JRC were trained for that sort of thing. He was just expected to operate some machines and occasionally act as a medic for the other JRCs.

Hatsumi lunged forward and thrust the needle into the nape of Demura's neck. Hatsumi's thumb hit the syringe plunger and twenty cubic centimeters of hydrogen cyanide was injected into the vertebral subclavian artery. The poison immediately spread to the major carotid and raced through the bloodstream to his brain.

Aware he was only a second or two from death, Demura twisted around and pointed the Magnum at the ash-white face of his assassin. Lieutenant Demura's last conscious thought was to squeeze the trigger. He heard the revolver roar and saw Hatsumi's face explode as a .357 slug ripped through it. Then Demura fell to the floor, dead.

PROFESSOR YOICHI FROWNED as he watched a detail of JRC soldiers dispose of the bodies of Lieutenant Demura and the four slain men. The corpses were dropped into a chute that led to a chemical incinerator located in the basement of the building. Sulfuric acid would dissolve the bodies.

"Are you going to lecture me about my folly in bringing the Kompei agent here?" Professor Oshimi asked quietly.

"What's done is done," Yoichi said with a sigh. "And you would not listen to me anyway."

"Of course I would, Ouzu," Oshimi replied with a shrug. "But we have other matters of greater importance to discuss."

With a sly smile, he added, "Changing the face of the world is not easy, my friend."

6

Keio Ohara and David McCarter watched the students of the Zembu Dojo practice martial-arts techniques. Two young men dressed in white *gi* uniforms struggled, trying to throw each other off balance. Hands pulled lapels and sleeves until one student swept his opponent's feet from the mat with a simple judo move that sent the man toppling to the padded surface.

Two other students wielded *bo* and *sai*. The man with the *bo*—the long fighting stave—swung and jabbed with his stick, while the other student defended himself with a pair of *sai*—a short swordlike weapon with an 18-inch-long center blade and two curved prongs extending from the quillion. He managed to trap the stick between the center blade and a prong of one *sai* as he thrust the point of the other weapon at the stick man's throat.

Another pair of students were involved in a free-spar karate match, executing fundamental punches and kicks. Instructors, with black belts knotted around their waists, supervised the matches. Other students were busy striking sand-filled bags to temper hands and feet. A few others performed karate *kata*—a dancelike practice form—while three novices hammered and stabbed with wooden *boken* swords at a kendo dummy.

Keio shook his head with disapproval. A devoted martial artist, he was a third *dan* black belt in judo and a fifth *dan* in karate, and he had excelled in kendo, a form of Japanese fencing. The Zembu Dojo was not concerned with the heart of martial arts, a philosophy that teaches self-control, humility, respect for life and proper manners while training a person to unite body, mind and spirit.

"This looks more like a bleeding training camp for hand-to-hand combat than a dojo," McCarter muttered.

Keio smiled, pleased that his British partner had also noticed the crude unprincipled style of the so-called martial-arts school. "Perhaps the terrorists are using this place for exactly that purpose."

"Kohnichi wa," one of the dojo's instructors greeted, bowing at McCarter and Keio. "I am Shikimi Yoto. May I help you?"

"Kohnichi wa, sensei," Ohara replied, addressing the man as "teacher." "This is Carter-*san* from England. He is a news reporter for the BBC. I am his guide and translator, Matsu Kino."

"I am honored to meet you both," Shikimi said. "But why would the BBC be interested in this most humble dojo?"

"The BBC wants to do a documentary feature about Nippon," Keio explained. "Carter-*san* is searching for a worthy school of martial arts to feature in his story. The Zembu Dojo—the 'Total Dojo'—seemed an ideal choice.''

"You honor us, Matsu-*san*.'' Shikimi bowed. "But we do not seek such publicity. This is a rather exclusive school and we. . . .''

"Ee-ya!" an angry voice barked.

Everyone present turned to see a powerfully built figure clad in a black *gi* with a *boken* thrust through an *obi* sash knotted around his waist. Instructors and students quickly bowed to the man in black.

He barely nodded in reply. His gaze immediately fell upon Keio and McCarter. The man's face was as impassive as a wooden samurai war mask, yet his black eyes burned with furious energy. Although he was clearly the *ichibahn sensei* of the dojo, the man appeared to be no older than thirty-two, quite young to command such respect.

"Daito-*san*," Shikimi called to him. *"Nan-no kosho desu kah?"*

But Daito-*san* did not tell him what was wrong. He ignored Shikimi and strode purposefully toward the three students who had been practicing swordsmanship on the kendo dummy.

"Kimi," Daito snarled at the trio. *"Kogeki!"*

The three novices were startled by the *sensei*'s order to attack, but they quickly obeyed. The closest man raised his *boken* over his head in a two-handed grip and charged Daito. Moving with catlike grace and incredible speed, the man in black stepped aside. His wooden sword became a blur as Daito drew the *boken* in a lightning-fast *iai-jutsu* stroke, chopping the rock-maple blade across the student's forearm. The novice cried out and dropped his sword, clutching his forearm with his other hand.

Daito moved smoothly and immediately dealt with the second attacker. The student had raised his *boken*, but Daito executed a *do* stroke, and the wooden blade of his sword slammed into the man's abdomen. The novice gasped and sunk to his knees as the third student attacked, his *boken* held high.

The *sensei* deftly stepped forward and caught one of the student's wrists and pivoted, twisting his opponent's arm. The novice suddenly plunged head over heels from the skillful *katate-nage* throw and crashed to the hardwood floor, unprotected by a judo mat. Daito's *boken* cracked against the floor next to the man's ear to simulate a lethal stroke to the head.

"He's damn good," McCarter whispered.

"Yeah," Keio agreed, surprised to see such a skilled demonstration of *kenjutsu*, the most combative style of Japanese fencing, in such a sorry excuse for a dojo.

"I do not wish to be rude," Shikimi told them. "But I must return to my class."

"Of course, *sensei*," Ohara replied. "We shall have to find another dojo for the BBC to film. Please excuse this intrusion."

"May you find better fortune elsewhere, Matsu-*san*," Shikimi said with a deep bow.

Keio and McCarter returned the gesture and left the dojo. Daito-*san* marched across the room to a window and watched the pair approach a blue Honda coupe.

"Follow them," Daito ordered.

"The foreigner is a British television reporter and the other man—" Shikimi began.

"I said, follow them," Daito insisted. "Our men can keep in contact by car radio. Take no chances with those two."

"Wakari-masin," the puzzled Shikimi said. "I do not understand. Do you think these men are dangerous?"

"You failed to notice the bulge under the European's left arm," Daito growled. "Why does this television reporter carry a gun?"

He turned to the students. *"Ikimas. Isogu,"* Daito ordered sharply, slashing his hand through the air. *"Ima."*

Heads quickly bowed in reply and the students bolted from the dojo. Some dashed to the locker room connected to the gym to change into street clothes. Others ran outside to their cars, still clad in white *gis*.

The man known as Daito-*san* watched the others depart. He wished he could go with them. Daito relished personal combat, which he considered to be the most honest and pure of all man's activities. He would rather participate in the kill than coordinate battle strategy from the sidelines.

He was once called Masaaki Sakade, born to a warrior family. Sakades had been fighting men for centuries. His ancestors had served as samurai knight-warriors during the time of *daimyos* and shoguns. The Sakades had always been very proud of this tradition. The way of the sword had always been the religion of the Sakade family.

Masaaki's father had also been a twentieth-century samurai. He was an officer in the Japanese occupation forces in the Philippines during World War II. When the Americans defeated the Japanese in the Pacific, Captain Sakade boldly attacked a machine-gun nest with a pistol in one hand and a sword in the other until a blast of automatic fire ripped bullets into both his legs.

A U.S. medical team treated the wounded warrior. When Sakade awoke from a morphine-induced slumber, he found his right leg was missing. The American translator claimed the leg was too badly damaged to save and they had been forced to amputate. Sakade never believed this, convinced that the barbarians had crippled him for life as a form of sadistic punishment. Masaaki would later inherit this hatred for Americans from his father.

Raised on warrior propaganda, *kenjutsu* lessons and hatred for the United States and the other Western powers, Sakade was a perfect candidate for a terrorist organization. In 1968 he was recruited by the Japanese Red Army. The fierce young man quickly learned the skills of an urban terrorist and soon became the commander of a JRA group that specialized in strike missions within Nippon and Okinawa.

Sakade led his band of fanatics on some of the most destructive and bloody operations in the history of terrorism. Even by the Red Army's standards, Sakade was a daring and vicious "soldier against oppression.'' His superiors admired Sakade's courage and cunning, but they worried that his boldness might make him careless.

In the early 1970s the Japanese authorities hunted down the JRA like hungry cats searching for rats in a barn. Sakade and many other terrorist leaders managed to escape capture by fleeing the country. Some, like Tanaga Zeko, ran to South Yemen. Others, including Sakade, headed for the closest Communist ally: North Korea.

In Korea, Sakade met Professor Ouzu Yoichi who was attempting to put together a new terrorist organization called the Japanese Red Cell. The Communist professor had connections with the Russian KGB and the North Korean UNGII, which would help furnish weapons, but most of the finances would come from an even more mysterious source.

When Yoichi explained the plans for the JRC to Sakade, the terrorist eagerly joined the new outfit. Only then did he learn about Professor Edward Oshimi, the real mastermind behind the organization. Sakade was apprehensive about working with a Japanese American until he met Oshimi in person.

"I understand you hate Americans, Sakade-*san*," Oshimi remarked when they first met.

The terrorist warrior nodded.

"So do I," Oshimi stated.

"Do you hate yourself, Oshimi-*san*?" Sakade asked bluntly. "If so, I suggest *seppuku*, ritual suicide."

"If my American blood could be drained from

me," Oshimi began, "then I would gladly use a blade
to be rid of it. If I did not think we could defeat the
American oppressors and restore our country to the
greatness that was once Japan, I would indeed take
my own life. Yet, why should I do our enemies such a
favor?"

"You speak well," Sakade said simply.

"But words do not impress you, samurai?"
Oshimi smiled. "Very well. You will see actions as
well. I will need you to return to Japan to command
the JRC forces there. Since you are wanted by the
authorities, you will receive a new identity. You will
undergo plastic surgery and receive new identification papers and a new name. Even your comrades
will not know you by the name you were born with.
From this day on you shall be known as Daito-
san—Man of the Long Sword."

Daito served his new masters well. A zealot, a living weapon in human form, Daito was the perfect
terrorist. Fearless, ruthless and deadly, he would
carry out any mission regardless of danger to himself
or to innocent bystanders.

To Daito, danger was an abstract concept because
life and death are merely two sides of the same coin
of Fate. The terrorist's black-and-white view of the
world left no room for innocence of any kind, either
for himself or in others. Daito believed one either en-
dorsed the same twisted philosophy as his or one was
an enemy who deserved an abrupt violent death.

Daito never questioned the morality of the cause
he was so fanatically dedicated to. He was not even

concerned about the possibility of failure. Daito did not want a long life. An aged feeble warrior is a useless creature, a lion without claws or fangs that is best put out of its suffering.

Although Daito had no religion and believed in no god, he would have agreed with the New Testament passage that states, he who lives by the sword shall perish by it.

Daito would not have wanted it any other way.

RAFAEL ENCIZO AND IKEDA KEN entered the manager's office of the Hoshiro Company. A short portly man, with gray-tinged sideburns and a whisk-broom mustache decorating his otherwise bland face, rose from behind a small metal desk.

"*Kohnichi wa.* I am Satsu Hoshiro," he declared in English with a curt bow. "The owner and manager of this company. How may I assist you?"

"This is Ricardo Rodriguez," Ikeda explained, using Rafael's cover name. "He is an investigator for an American insurance firm, specializing in claims concerning ships and security for vessels. I am Yawata Zento of Sekai Enterprises, an international import-export corporation located in Yokohama. We have done business with Mr. Rodriguez before. He is a most impressive professional."

"I'm certain that is true," Hoshiro said. "On the phone you said you had a business proposition for me."

"Security is a vital part of any business these days," Rafael explained. "I mean no disrespect,

Hoshiro-*san*, but your shipyards suffer certain flaws in this matter.''

"I own a small fishing fleet,'' the manager answered. ''Sabotage is hardly a problem I need to consider.''

"But your boats are vulnerable to thieves,'' the Cuban stated. ''I took the liberty of looking over your fishing fleet. A thief could easily board any vessel by simply climbing over a gunwale. The doors to the cabins appear to be secured by simple button locks that can be opened with a credit card.''

"Several of my stevedores patrol the docks after dark, Mr. Rodriguez,'' Hoshiro said. ''They are strong men and they carry clubs. It would be most unwise for a thief to attempt to steal one of my boats....''

Knuckles rapped on the door before it opened. A huge figure lumbered across the threshold and bowed before Hoshiro. He was less than six feet tall, but his bulk seemed to fill the doorway. Rafael guessed the man's weight to be more than three hundred pounds. Much of this was fat, but the muscular development of his massive shoulders, thick arms and tree-trunk legs clearly indicated that considerable strength lurked within his flabby frame.

"Ah,'' Hoshiro said, smiling, ''this is Tado-*san*. He is my chief of security, in charge of the protection of my property. Tado-*san* was formerly a sumo wrestler. Not the sort of man any thief would care to confront.''

"*Junsa koko*, Hoshiro-*san*," the sumo stated grimly.

"*Desho juyonai,*" Hoshiro replied, his tone seeming casual, but his expression revealing alarm. "*Matteh kudasai*, Tado-*san*."

"*Wakari-masu,*" the Japanese hulk said, nodding.

"The police are here," Hoshiro explained for Rafael's benefit. "I'm certain it isn't important, but I'd better talk to them. Will you excuse me?"

"Certainly," Ikeda assured him.

Hoshiro hurried from the office, followed by Tado. Ikeda moved to the door and watched the pair descend a flight of stairs to the storage room below.

"I hope the cops don't scare these guys into a gunfight," Rafael commented as he walked to a filing cabinet near the desk.

"The police will be subtle," Ikeda assured him, but he unbuttoned his jacket to allow easy access to the Nambu pistol in a shoulder holster under his arm. "They will only ask Hoshiro if he knows the whereabouts of one of the terrorists from the airport who had been in his employ. Since the incident occurred in Tokyo and these are local police, Hoshiro will have no reason to react in a drastic manner to their questions."

"I hope you're right," the Cuban remarked, removing a small leather package from a pocket. "We wouldn't stand a chance if all the Hoshiro personnel around here charge out with guns blazing."

He took two slender steel probes from the pack and inserted them in the cabinet's keyhole. The lock was a single-tumbler model, and he had no trouble picking it. Rafael slid open a drawer and nodded at Ikeda.

"You'd better look at the files," the Cuban suggested as he changed places with the Kompei chief. "I doubt if they're written in Spanish or English."

While Rafael stationed himself at the door, Ikeda quickly leafed through the file folders. Much of the information he found consisted of recent catches of fish and market sales. However, Ikeda discovered something of interest. He extracted a small camera, no larger than a pack of cigarettes, and photographed several sheets before returning the files.

"We probably don't have much time, Ken," Rafael reminded him.

"I know," the Japanese agreed. "Better lock this cabinet for now...although I think we'll want to come back for a better look at the rest of these records later."

"What did you find?" Rafael asked, again trading places with Ikeda.

"Enough," the Kompei man answered. "Hoshiro has lists of cities with the numbers of 'troops' stationed at each locale. These are ranked as first, second and third. The Zembu Dojo is a second-level base."

"Let's get out of here," Rafael said as he twisted the lock picks in the cabinet until the latch clicked into place. "With only one squad car of cops for backup, we're not in any position to tangle with these guys. Hell, the police don't even carry guns here ex-

cept in an emergency. . . providing they know about
the emergency in advance.''

"We'll return with reinforcements," Ikeda said.
"*Armed* reinforcements, and arrest Hoshiro and the
others.''

"Not yet," Rafael urged. "This place can't be the
headquarters for the entire Red Cell. There are still
bigger fish to catch, my friend.''

"What do you suggest?" Ikeda asked.

"Let's check on Keio and McCarter," the Cuban
replied. "I want to be certain they returned from
their visit to a 'second-level terrorist base'—whatever
the hell that means.''

"Very well," Ikeda sighed. "But I hope you don't
expect Kompei to wait very long. My superiors tend
to get impatient.''

"Don't worry about that," Rafael told him. "My
associates and I are just as eager to put these terrorists out of business as you are.''

He smiled coldly as he added, "We're going to
make sure the Red Cell bleeds to death.''

7

"It's been so bloody long I've almost forgotten how to use these things," David McCarter commented as he plunged a pair of chopsticks into a plate of suki-yaki.

"Perhaps we should have gone somewhere less traditional," Keio Ohara commented.

The Tengoku restaurant was very "Japanese." There were no chairs. Customers knelt on tatami mats by low tables. The walls and doors of the dining room were made of paper screens. The waitresses wore kimonos in the manner of geisha.

A small rock garden with multicolored stones arranged in the patterns of Zen symbols dominated the center of the room. The only Western object in the restaurant was a small umbrella stand in a corner by the door.

McCarter was the only Occidental customer in the dining room, yet no one stared at the European. Such behavior would not have been *enryo*.

"No," the Briton assured Keio. "This will be fine."

The Japanese member of Phoenix Force smiled. He recalled that McCarter had spent many years in

Shanghai and Hong Kong as an SAS soldier, as well as time in Laos and Vietnam with an "observation" team attached to American SOG Intelligence. McCarter was often impatient, short-tempered and overemotional, but he was no stranger to the Orient, and the tranquil atmosphere seemed to bring another part of his personality to the surface.

"You're sure Rafael can find his way here?" McCarter asked, sipping *cha* tea—wishing it was Coca-Cola.

"When he contacted us by CB radio, Ikeda was with him," Keio replied. "I'm certain he won't have any trouble."

"I hope Gary and Yakov have been able to get those damn crates out of the airport cargo section," McCarter commented. "I'll be glad to get my hands on familiar weapons again."

He still carried the Nambu pistol he had taken from a dead JRC terrorist at the airport. Unlike the old World War II model, which resembled a German Luger in 8mm caliber, the new Nambu featured a Browning-style frame and fired 9mm ammo. Keio's .44 AutoMag was too big to conceal under his jacket, so he still carried it in the briefcase that sat beside him as he knelt by the table.

"Gary and Yakov are more experienced in matters of diplomacy and business than the rest of us," Ohara said. "I'm sure...."

The screen door suddenly slid open and four figures dressed in sweat shirts, slacks and stocking masks burst into the dining room. Two of the invaders carried Skorpion machine pistols. Another held a Makarov in one hand and a bloodstained bayonet in the other. The curves of the fourth terrorist's body revealed her sex, but a North Korean M-68 pistol in her hand warned that she was as deadly as her male comrades.

"Bleedin' hell," McCarter groaned when he stared up at the muzzle of a silenced machine pistol.

"Nani gah iri-masu?" a waitress asked, trembling as she bowed before the terrorists.

None of the Japanese Red Cell savages told her what they wanted, but the goon with the Makarov stepped forward and smashed the barrel of his pistol across the girl's face. She fell to the tatami mats, blood oozing from her mouth.

McCarter stiffened with anger, but the Skorpion kept him nailed to the spot. Keio slowly moved a hand toward his briefcase. The female terrorist hooked a foot around the case and kicked it out of Ohara's reach as she aimed her pistol at his head.

Customers cried out in alarm and fear. The second man with a sound-suppressed machine pistol demanded silence by blasting a spray of 7.65mm slugs into a trio of Japanese patrons. The noise suppressor shuddered, and two businessmen and a middle-aged secretary convulsed in agony as the bullets plowed through their flesh.

A woman screamed in the kitchen. Her cry ended abruptly. Two more terrorists entered the dining room. One carried a pistol, the other held a *waka-*

zashi—a samurai short sword. The razor-sharp blade dripped crimson.

"Who send you, American?" the JRC thug, who had slugged the waitress, demanded in broken English.

"Figure the odds will be better outside?" McCarter muttered to Keio.

"You want these goons to suck information out of us?" Ohara replied.

McCarter understood. If the JRC picked their brains, the terrorists would learn details about Phoenix Force. Yakov, Manning and Rafael would be in mortal danger. Stony Man Farm itself would be jeopardized, and the true identity of Colonel Phoenix would fall into the hands of the enemy. McCarter and Keio considered these secrets to be more important than their own lives.

"Then let's see how many of these bastards we can take with us," the Briton whispered.

"Yes," Ohara said, glancing up at the female savage who stood over him.

"Answer, American," the terrorist spokesman snapped.

"I'm not a bleedin' Yank, damn it," McCarter replied sharply. "I'm a citizen of the United Kingdom and an employee of the British Broadcasting Corporation. I'll show you my passport if that will make you happy...."

"No passport," the thug growled. "You come. *Ima!*"

"My name isn't Ema," McCarter scoffed as he

rose to his feet. "Good God, man. What do you think I am? Irish or something?"

The man with the Skorpion stepped closer and gestured with his weapon. McCarter glanced at the other terrorists. The woman was still standing next to Keio. Two thugs were positioned at each door. The other machine gunner covered the customers who had survived the first blast of gunfire. A pistol-packing JRC killer decided to inspect Keio's briefcase while the sword-wielding barbarian stood in the center of the room, apparently waiting for another chance to use his *wakazashi*.

"Don't do anything rash," McCarter urged as he lowered his right hand toward his jacket.

"Ee-ya," the man with the Skorpion warned.

"It's just my passport, for—"

McCarter's left hand suddenly shot out, swatting the Skorpion away from himself as he yanked the Nambu from shoulder leather. The terrorist automatically pulled the trigger of his machine pistol that hoarsely barked through its sound suppressor. The female member of the JRC killer squad screamed as four 7.65mm rounds ripped into her chest.

McCarter quickly stabbed the muzzle of his Nambu into the Skorpion gunner's midsection and squeezed the trigger. A 9mm bullet blasted a tunnel of destruction through the man's solar plexus and xiphoid cartilage, breaking the sixth thoracic vertebra before it burst out his back. Terrorist weapons turned toward the Briton as McCarter hit the floor. A volley of gunfire hissed above his prone form.

Keio had already leaped into the melee—literally. He grabbed the only available weapons, his chopsticks, and lunged over the table. Ohara's desperate, furious action caught the terrorists off guard—especially the group's spokesman who suddenly found Keio on top of him.

A forearm smash knocked the Makarov from the JRC sadist's grasp. Before he could use the bayonet in his other hand, Keio's right arm turned into a bolt of deadly lightning. The terrorist shrieked and staggered backward with a chopstick buried in his left eyesocket. The wooden tip had pierced the eyeball and punctured the man's brain.

McCarter fired the Nambu pistol from a prone position on the tatami mats, ignoring the frightened cries of restaurant customers and the angry shouts of startled terrorists. The center of a JRC hitman's mask exploded as a 9mm slug sliced through his head. Propelled backward by the impact of the bullet, the man's body crashed through the flimsy paper-and-bamboo screen of a sliding door.

Keio delivered a fast roundhouse kick and sent a pistol flying from another terrorist's broken fingers. The man howled in terror and pain. Then Keio thrust the other chopstick into the hollow of the man's throat. The piece of human filth vomited blood and wilted to the floor.

"Haiii!" the sword-swinging killer cried as he charged, slashing his *wakazashi* at Ohara's head.

The remaining terrorist snapped a hasty shot at McCarter and fled from the dining room. He met

four other members of the Japanese Red Cell who had
been waiting outside the restaurant in a television-
repair truck and a minibus until the sound of gunfire
convinced them their services were needed inside.

"¡MADRE DE DIOS!" Rafael Encizo exclaimed.

The Cuban and Ikeda Ken had just pulled up to the
Tengohu Restaurant in time to see four heavily
armed figures, clad in coveralls and stocking masks,
dash toward the building. The Kompei agent abruptly parked his Toyota behind the minibus. Rafael
popped open the passenger door and leaped from the
car before it came to a full stop.

A JRC triggerman saw the Cuban rush forward
with a Russian Makarov—another memento from
the carnage at the airport—in his hands. The terrorist
swung a 12-gauge pump shotgun with a cut-down
barrel at Rafael. The Makarov snarled, and a 9mm
bullet drilled into the man's masked face, right between the eyes. The terrorist fell backward and
blasted a load of buckshot into the night before he
crashed to the sidewalk and died.

"Abunai!" growled another terrorist as he turned
to point a Russian Stetchin machine pistol at Rafael.

A veteran at staying alive during violent encoun-
ters, the Cuban had already dashed to the cover of
the TV-repair truck before the JRC machine gunner
opened fire. Nine-millimeter bullets chewed into the
body of the truck and shattered two windows, but
none struck their intended target.

The terrorist not only failed to waste Rafael but he

also stepped across the threshold of the restaurant and presented Ikeda with a perfect target. The Kompei chief took advantage of the opportunity and carefully aimed his Nambu before squeezing off two shots. One ricocheted off the frame of the Stetchin and hit the JRC assassin in the face, cracking his cheekbone. He spun around from the unexpected blow and turned just in time to catch the second Nambu round with his chest.

As the JRC machine gunner crumbled to the sidewalk, another kill-crazy gunner fired a stolen U.S. Army Colt 1911A1 at Ikeda. The terrorist put a bullet in the Toyota's windshield instead of Ikeda. Rafael aimed his Makarov around the front fender of the repair truck and pumped a 9mm round into the side of the JRC flunky's head.

The two remaining terrorists in the restaurant foyer saw their comrade's skull burst apart in a spray of brains and bone fragments. They recoiled from the doorway in horror, uncertain of what to do next. David McCarter solved that problem for one of the bastards. He fired his Nambu from the dining room and put a 9mm slug between the terrorist's shoulder blades.

The wounded man groaned, stumbled, then fell flat on his face, his backbone broken. Panic-stricken, the other JRC fanatic whirled and fired his M-68 pistol. Two 7.65mm rounds smacked into a wall six feet from McCarter's position.

Suddenly, Rafael appeared at the front door. The lone terrorist turned to face him—too late. The

Cuban's Makarov snarled twice. David McCarter also opened fire at the same instant. Four slugs crashed into the man's chest, tearing his heart and lungs to pieces. The terrorist fell to the floor and one more JRC member was on his way to hell.

KEIO OHARA had managed to dodge the slashing blade of his opponent's *wakazashi* and leaped to the umbrella stand in the corner of the room. Keio quickly grabbed a flimsy umbrella. The JRC killer attacked.

Keio slammed the umbrella into the flat of his adversary's blade and stopped the sword stroke. The startled terrorist quickly tried to thrust the slanted point of his *wakazashi* into Keio's chest, but the agile Phoenix Force pro sidestepped. Restaurant patrons watched in amazement as Keio moved in and rapped the bamboo handle of the umbrella on the assassin's wrist, striking the ulna nerve.

The sword dropped from numb fingers, and Keio quickly swung the umbrella around, hooking the handle on his opponent's neck. Ohara pivoted, bent at the waist and pulled the umbrella. The terrorist was yanked forward and adroitly thrown over Keio's hip.

The hoodlum landed in the center of the rock garden, his back making hard contact with the stone Zen symbols. Ohara stomped a heel into the man's stomach. The terrorist spewed life. Keio pulled on the umbrella with his right hand. The handle was still hooked around the thug's neck. The terrorist's head rose swiftly to meet Keio's fist. The *seiken* punch, delivered with the first two big knuckles of his left hand, crashed between the man's eyes.

The terrorist's body went limp, and Keio unhooked the umbrella from his opponent's neck. The awestruck civilians watched with horror as Keio reversed his grip on the umbrella and forcibly drove its metal point into the man's chest. The bullet tip punched into the sternal notch, cracking and penetrating the breastbone. Blood spurted from the hideous wound. The umbrella had found a new stand—lodged in the dead man's chest.

David McCarter and Rafael Encizo entered the dining room to see Keio gather up the *wakazashi* in one hand and his briefcase in the other. The terrified restaurant patrons saw the guns in the fists of the two Occidentals. They cowered back against the walls, still fearful that karma had decided their time on earth had run out.

"I thought you said this was a quiet little restaurant," Rafael remarked dryly as he thrust his pistol into its shoulder holster.

8

Gary Manning and Yakov Katzenelenbogen met McCarter, Rafael, Keio and Ikeda at the Kompei chief's office. This time Ikeda offered everyone sake instead of tea.

"The incident at the restaurant was very bad," Ikeda said sadly. "So many died."

"Weep for the innocent, my friend," Rafael stated bluntly. "The Japanese Red Cell is a cancer. Killing them is simply preventing a disease from becoming an epidemic."

"Violence should be used only as a last resort," the Kompei agent insisted as he poured himself another cup of sake.

"That's true," Yakov agreed. The Israeli now wore his favorite prosthetic device. He gestured with the steel hook at the end of his right arm as he spoke. "But violence is always the *first* resort of terrorism. That leaves us only one logical choice of action. One *last* resort."

Ikeda shook his head. "Perhaps you are right. I myself said we must do whatever's necessary to stop the Red Cell. Yet, I am troubled that such tactics are not unlike those of the terrorists themselves."

"Wait a minute," Rafael told him. "The JRC murdered unarmed civilians in cold blood. That, Ikeda-*san*, is the difference."

"*Hai,*" the Kompei agent said, nodding. "Yes, and we acted in self-defense. I, too, killed a man this night."

"We brought the crates of equipment from the airport," Manning said quickly, wanting to change the subject. "You fellas want your toys now?"

"Hell, yes," McCarter replied eagerly.

Gary Manning placed a suitcase on the coffee table. Rafael and McCarter were standing by his side when he snapped open the case. The Cuban immediately took a Gerber Mark I boot knife from the open luggage.

He smiled as he drew the dagger from its sheath. An excellent fighting knife, the Gerber features a five-inch, double-edged-steel blade and a cast aluminum handle with a full quillion. Rafael never felt comfortable without his pet knife, which had saved his life many times.

McCarter was equally attached to his personal weapons and quickly reclaimed his Browning Hi-Power autoloader and Bianchi shoulder holster. The Briton removed his sports jacket and slipped into the leather rig.

"Yes, I feel better now," he commented as he inserted a magazine into the Browning and worked the slide to chamber the first 9mm rounds. "I couldn't shoot that bloody Nambu worth a damn."

McCarter fished his Ingram M-10 machine pistol

from the case while Rafael claimed a Walther PPK and an H&K MP-5 SD3. A compact, 9mm machine pistol, the Heckler & Koch resembled an AR-7 with a folding stock and a cut-down barrel. However, the MP-5 weapons were equipped with built-in silencers and special sights for additional accuracy, a weak point in most silenced weapons. The weapon was a favorite of the West German GSG-9 antiterrorist department.

Although Rafael preferred to use a Stoner submachine gun, the H&K had been more practical to transport via a commercial airplane and better suited for close-quarters combat.

"Keio," Katzenelenbogen began, "what sort of arms do you have access to besides that elephant gun you call a pistol?"

"An Ingram M-10," the Japanese team member replied. He had been quietly cleaning and sharpening the blade of the *wakazashi*. "An M-16 assault rifle with a 203 grenade-launcher attachment, a forty-five 1911A1 Colt and an assorted collection of grenades."

"Better bring the M-16 with the 203," the Israeli advised. "We might need a long-range weapon tonight."

"Tonight?" Ikeda asked with surprise. "What are you planning to do?"

"The JRC is bound to go underground now," McCarter explained. "That means we've got to hit them before they get a chance to slip away."

"Most of the weapons used by the terrorists have

been imported from Communist countries," Yakov explained. "That means they have connections with other international terrorist outfits or a direct link with the Russians. If we give them enough time, they're apt to flee Japan and head for a terrorist training camp in the Middle East or North Korea."

"They could even wind up in the Soviet Union," Keio added as he slid the *wakazashi* into its black-lacquered wood scabbard.

"Just a moment," Ikeda began. "The Tokyo police have been most agreeable with us thus far, but even Kompei can't ask them to ignore another bloodbath— not after what's already happened tonight."

"We won't be in Tokyo," Yakov assured him.

"The Hoshiro Company?" Ikeda frowned.

"It's a major base for the JRC," Manning remarked.

"What about the Zembu Dojo?" McCarter inquired. "That must be where Keio and I attracted enough attention to convince the bastards to send a hit team to the restaurant after us."

"The dojo is too small to be very important," Yakov said. "And the JRC wouldn't dare have a main headquarters in the heart of Tokyo. The city is too densely populated. Security would be too difficult with so many eyes and ears around."

"But we have no idea how many terrorists are stationed at the Hoshiro Company," Ikeda insisted. "There could be a hundred waiting there."

"Then there will be a hundred *less* to worry about after tonight," Rafael remarked with a shrug.

9

Aaron Palmer rode in the back seat of the limousine with two of his agents beside him. The vehicle was driven by a Kompei officer. Another Japanese Intel man rode "shotgun" in the front seat.

A second vehicle, a gray sedan filled with Japanese commandos trained in antiterrorist tactics, brought up the rear. Four policemen, mounted on Honda motorcycles, escorted the cars—two *junsa* in the front and two behind.

"When will we reach Chiba?" Palmer asked the Kompei agent seated beside the driver.

"Very soon, Parmer-*san*," Agent Yashedi replied.

Palmer smiled. The guy pronounced his name as if it was a type of cheese. What the hell, Palmer thought. Yashedi's English was still a lot better than his Japanese.

"Christ," Agent Brown, seated beside Palmer, muttered. "I've never heard of Chiba before."

"That's why we're going there instead of Tokyo," Agent Morton explained. "Kompei is a good intel company. They know what they're doing."

Morton had formerly been stationed as a U.S. agent-in-place in Japan. He knew the country, the customs, the language and the people. That is why he had been chosen to accompany Palmer on the trip.

When their plane had landed at Tokyo International Airport, Kompei agents and policemen were waiting for the three Americans. An alarming rash of terrorist activity had prompted the Japanese authorities to alter plans for Palmer's visit.

They had decided to take Palmer directly to Chiba, a small city southeast of Tokyo. Terrorists tend to conduct most of their operations in major cities, so Chiba seemed an ideal place for the American VIP.

The motorcade, however, canceled any chance for a clandestine move. Two large cars with a police escort had VIP written all over it. Kompei seemed to think secrecy was not as important as the additional firepower provided by the commandos.

If the Japanese Red Cell had planned to hit Palmer at the airport, they would be apt to cancel the attempt because of the odds they would have to take on.

Motorcades, however, are not invulnerable to assassins or terrorists. President Kennedy had been killed by a sniper when he had ridden through the streets of Dallas; General Haig had nearly been blown to bits when a bomb exploded on a road in Belgium; USAEUR—United States Army in Europe—commander, General Kroezer, narrowly escaped death from a rocket launcher in West Germany; Aldo Moro's motorcade had been stopped by a road blockade. Red Brigades terrorists gunned down the former Italian premier's bodyguards and kidnapped Moro, who was later found dead.

Every man in the motorcade to Chiba was aware of these incidents. They watched the surrounding area for any signs of danger. Agent Morton drew a Smith & Wesson Model 59 from shoulder leather and jacked a 9mm cartridge into the chamber. Brown, basically a paper pusher, had left his gun in a suitcase that had been locked in the trunk of the limo. All the Japanese were armed. Even the motorcycle cops carried riot guns in saddle boots on their Hondas.

Everyone sighed with relief when they arrived at Chiba without encountering any obstacles.

Although much smaller than Tokyo, Chiba is a modern city with high-rise apartment towers, office buildings and a steadily growing population. Many residents of Chiba commute to Tokyo or work at the local harbors. In time Chiba will probably become part of Tokyo, since the capital of Japan continues to grow, swallowing suburbs, turning everything into a massive metropolis.

The motorcade arrived at the Migato hotel. A squad of policemen, both Tokyo and Chiba officers, had blocked off a space in front of the hotel for the vehicles. The motorcade pulled up at the curb. Cops dismounted from motorcycles and exchanged salutes and bows with fellow officers. Car doors opened and policemen saluted Palmer and his party.

Agent Morton emerged from the limo and asked the police about the security measures taken. Aaron Palmer and Yashedi joined them. Then Agent Brown climbed out of the car.

His skull exploded.

Blood and brains splattered Palmer and Morton. Yashedi and several policemen shouted orders. The commandos leaped from the sedan, M-16 rifles held ready. One of the troopers fell to the sidewalk, a large bloody hole in the center of his chest.

"Asoko," voices cried as fingers pointed at the dull glint of a muzzle-flash from a silencer-equipped rifle on the roof of the building across the street from the Migato hotel.

Commandos instantly moved behind the cover of parked cars and opened fire. The metallic chatter of automatic rifles filled the night as streams of 5.56mm rounds poured into the sniper's position. A figure toppled from the roof and fell to the pavement, his body ripped and mangled by bullets.

Three police officers hastily escorted Palmer and Morton into the hotel, while other cops and Kompei agents scattered to check surrounding buildings for more terrorists. Palmer and his group entered the hotel lobby where five uniformed policemen waited.

"Iras-shai," a hard-faced cop ordered as he led the way down a corridor to the emergency fire stairs.

"Matteh!" snapped an officer dressed in a Tokyo

police lieutenant's uniform. He frowned at the other cop. *"Do sh'te—"*

The lieutenant never finished his sentence. A white-gloved hand grabbed his mouth from behind as a "policeman" drove a knife blade into his left kidney.

Another killer clad in a cop uniform swung a wire garrote over an officer's head and twisted the steel cord around the man's neck. A cop, unaccustomed to carrying a side arm, clumsily clawed at a button-flap holster on his hip. He was suddenly seized from behind by another wolf in uniform who rammed a knee into the small of his back. Before the startled officer could react, the knife artist who had killed the lieutenant thrust his blade into the cop's heart.

A harsh metallic cough erupted, and Palmer turned to see Morton's right eyeball pop from its socket as a 7.65mm bullet splintered his cheekbone. One of the assassins in blue had shot him in the back of the head with a silenced M-68 pistol.

Aaron Palmer was unable to tell which cops were real and which were terrorists. Then the leader of the enemy hit team slammed a rock-hard *seiken* punch into Palmer's solar plexus. The American doubled up with a gasp and Daito-*san* hit him again, chopping the edge of his hand into the facial nerve under Palmer's jawbone. The American slumped unconscious to the floor.

"Good work, comrades," Daito told his fellow terrorists. "Takamine. Zuikaku. Take care of the bodies. Doyykai. Yamada. Guard the corridor. Harou, help me carry the capitalist *inu* downstairs.''

The terrorists quickly obeyed. Morton and the three slain policemen were dragged into an elevator. One of the killers pressed the button for the fifth floor, while his partner attached a long wire to the pin of a Soviet F-1 hand grenade and braced it under two corpses.

They stepped from the elevator and tied the other end of the wire to the stem of a metal ashtray mounted on the wall. The doors hummed shut and the elevator rose, pulling the wire taut. When the lift reached the second floor, the wire yanked the pin from the grenade.

The F-1 exploded between the third and fourth floors, blasting apart the elevator car, severing the hoist cables and breaking the roller guide and steel sling. What remained of the elevator crashed to the bottom of the shaft.

The explosion drew the police and Kompei agents from the street. They rushed to the stairwell and raced to the fourth floor. The JRC hitmen had already descended the stairs to the underground parking lot. Two patrol cars filled with phony police officers pulled onto the street, sirens screaming.

Other police cars and fire engines were racing to the Migato hotel. No one paid much attention to the pair of cop cars that sped away from the scene. Daito-*san*, seated in the back of one of the stolen vehicles, placed his feet on the helpless figure of

Aaron Palmer, who lay bound and gagged on the floor.

"You have much to tell us, American," Daito said with a cold smile. "And you will tell us everything we want to know. All the secrets of your country... everything we need to destroy the United States of America."

10

Four stevedores patrolled the pier at the Hoshiro Company. Fog clung to the harbor, creating an ominous atmosphere. The muscular sentries resembled horror-film ghouls as they marched through the mist with thick clubs in hand. Each man also had a pistol and a fighting knife hidden under his wool jacket, and each was trained in crash courses of judo, karate and sumo wrestling.

One of the brutes stopped at the side of a storage shed and removed a pack of cigarettes from a coat pocket. He shook one out, placed it in his mouth and struck a match. Cupping a hand around the flame, he raised it to the cigarette.

Then something hard smashed into the base of his neck, breaking vertebrae on impact. The stevedore lived long enough to grunt, then he crumbled to the plank walk. Muscle spasms caused his body to twitch. Gary Manning raised his H&K G3 SG1 rifle and stamped the butt into the back of the man's skull to be certain he would never rise again.

Another stevedore checked the door of the main office building. The guard then heard cloth rustle behind him. With a gasp, he began to turn. He was seized at the back of the neck. Steel talons squeezed forcibly, sharp points biting into flesh. The stevedore tried to scream, blood bubbling from his mouth. The hideous sound of crunching bone filled his ears. Then his spinal cord snapped.

Yakov Katzenelenbogen opened the steel claw at the end of his arm and lowered the corpse to the plank walk. He wiped the blades of his prosthetic arm on the dead man's jacket as Rafael Encizo approached. The Cuban nodded, acknowledging Yakov's success in silently taking out the sentry. The Israeli returned the gesture.

Another guard strolled around the corner of the building. He saw Yakov; he saw the Uzi submachine gun that hung from a strap on the Israeli's left shoulder. The sentry immediately reached for a pistol in his belt.

Rafael's H&K MP-5 rasped a three-round burst, and a triangle of bullet holes appeared in the sentry's upper chest. His sternum and manubrium pulverized, the JRC muscle boy was kicked backward by the impact of the multiple 9mm slugs. The man uttered a choked groan and fell to the pier.

The fourth and last guard heard his comrade's feeble moan. He pulled a Makarov from a shoulder holster and hurried toward the sound. The stevedore failed to notice the soft footfalls behind him as a tall shadow followed, holding a long steel blade in one fist.

Suddenly the sentry stopped. A sixth sense warned of danger, and he glanced over his shoulder in time to see a streak of silver lightning that struck the side of his neck.

Keio Ohara's *wakazashi* sliced through flesh, muscle and bone with a single stroke. The man's head fell to the plank walk. His decapitated corpse staggered toward Keio like a headless drunk. Aware a muscle reaction might trigger the pistol in the dead man's hand, Keio swung the sword again. The gun landed at Keio's feet, the severed hand still clenched around the weapon's grip.

The nightmare on two legs finally accepted death and slumped to the plank walk, blood still gushing from the stump of its neck and wrist. Keio stepped over the grisly corpse and hurried to join the other members of Phoenix Force, who had assembled by the office building.

"Hoshiro's office is located upstairs," Rafael explained as he inserted his lock picks into the keyhole of the door. "The downstairs is just a storage area...."

"Down," Manning said when he saw a figure at the starboard quarter of one of the fishing boats docked in the harbor.

Phoenix Force dropped to the plank walk as an AK-47 opened fire. Copper-jacketed projectiles splintered the wall above their prone bodies. Manning aimed his H&K SG1 at the gunman.

An infrared telescopic sight mounted on the barrel of the automatic rifle allowed Manning to easily locate the terrorist sniper. The cross hairs fell on the center of the killer's forehead. Manning squeezed the trigger and split the JRC hitman's skull with a 7.62mm bullet.

"Keio, McCarter," Yakov shouted. "Hit those boats."

McCarter and Ohara bolted for the fishing fleet as more terrorists appeared on the decks of three vessels. The Briton, armed with a short-range M-10 machine pistol, took the lead, while Keio supplied cover fire with his M-16. McCarter's silenced Ingram coughed, and a volley of 9mm rounds sent two JRC followers into a jitterbug of death.

The terrorists on board the other boats were uncertain where the gunman was because of the fog and the lack of muzzle-flash from his silenced weapon. Still, three JRC soldiers aimed guns in McCarter's direction.

Keio did not allow them to try their luck at shooting at the shadows. His M-16 snarled and slammed a salvo of 5.56mm slugs into the trio. One terrorist fell to his knees, both hands clamped over his bullet-gouged face. The other two were kicked over the rail for an impromptu funeral at sea.

"Screw picking the lock," Rafael muttered as he aimed his MP-5 at the door and blasted the lock with a three-round burst. The Cuban, Yakov and Manning all stood clear of the door. Rafael kicked it open. A shotgun bellowed, and a swarm of Number 6 pellets spat through the opening. Encizo poked his weapon around the edge of the doorway and fired a quick volley, while Manning removed a concussion grenade from his black ditty bag.

He yanked the pin and hurled the canister into the building. The grenade erupted. Glass burst from windows on the first floor. Manning and Rafael plunged inside to find half a dozen dazed terrorists sprawled on the floor, blood dripping from their nostrils and ears. Rafael terminated their suffering by hosing the wounded terrorists with 9mm rounds.

YAKOV WAS ABOUT TO FOLLOW the two younger men inside the building when four figures charged across the pier, heading for the Israeli. Katz dropped to one knee and braced his Uzi across his prosthetic arm. He squeezed the trigger and expertly chopped down three JRC zealots with hot blasts of destruction.

The fourth lunatic kept coming, blood oozing from four bullet wounds in his chest. The terrorist screamed a *kiya* battle cry as he swung a stevedore hook overhead.

Katz aimed the Uzi at the rampaging fanatic and fired once more, gradually elevating the barrel. Nine-millimeter slugs tore into the terrorist from navel to forehead. His body was hurtled across the pier by the force of the projectiles.

"*Haiii-ya!*" a voice bellowed.

Yakov turned to see that a JRC assassin had crept out of the fog to attack from behind. The assailant swung a long oak *bo* stave in a deadly arch aimed at Yakov's skull.

Katzenelenbogen's prosthetic arm rose in an overhead block. Wood smashed into steel. The terrorist gasped when he saw his white oak stave break in two when it struck Katz's arm. Then he felt the stubby barrel of the Uzi jab into his midsection. Yakov squeezed the trigger and nearly cut his opponent in two.

The submachine gun exhausted its ammunition. Before Yakov could swap magazines, another JRC killer charged forward, wielding a *nunchaku*. Katz had never met Shikimi Yoto, one of the martial-arts instructors at the Zembu Dojo... until now. Shikimi had waited for the right moment before launching his attack, confident he could defeat an older man armed only with an empty gun.

Yakov knew the *nunchaku*—an Okinawan weapon consisting of two sticks connected by a short chain— is far more lethal than it appears. A *nunchaku* stick travels at speeds greater than seventy-five miles per hour, and even a glancing blow can shatter bone. Shikimi's weapon sliced through the air in a vicious figure-eight pattern as the Israeli raised his Uzi.

The *nunchaku* bounced off the frame of the machine gun, whirled and struck again, only to connect with Yakov's prosthetic arm. The ex-Mossad agent delivered a low sidekick to his opponent's kneecap, breaking the patella bone in Shikimi's left leg.

Shikimi howled in pain, shocked that he had been a victim of one of the most fundamental karate techniques. His shattered leg buckled, and he fell to the plank walk. Yakov stepped back and pulled a .45-caliber Colt Commander from a shoulder holster under his right arm. Shikimi stared up to see the muzzle of the pistol before Yakov shot him in the face.

TWO JAPANESE RED CELL SAVAGES on board a fishing boat opened fire on Keio with AK-47 assault rifles. Ohara dived for cover behind a cargo crane. Bullets whined as they ricocheted off the framework of the steel hoist.

Keio returned fire with the M-203 grenade launcher attached to a sleeve on the barrel of his M-16. A fat HE projectile sailed across the pier and crashed into the fly bridge of the enemy vessel. The grenade exploded, blasting the boat into a pile of splintered, burning wreckage with charred human corpses among the debris.

David McCarter had climbed on board another boat, his Ingram blasting a terrorist as the hardguy emerged from the bulkhead. The Briton paused to swap magazines, then he heard footsteps on the fly bridge.

"You bastards aren't going anywhere," he hissed as he yanked the pin from an M-26 fragmentation grenade and lobbed it overhead.

He leaped over the transom and threw himself flat on the pier. A pistol cracked and a bullet splintered wood near the Briton's head.

The M-26 exploded and tore apart the fly bridge—including the two JRC flunkies who had been positioned there. Wood, glass and twisted metal spewed across the harbor. McCarter rolled to the shelter of a pile of crates and hastily reloaded his Ingram while

Keio Ohara launched a one-man raid on the last vessel in the Hoshiro fleet.

Keio spotted two terrorists at the foredeck who had just removed an American M-60 machine gun from the cabin trunk. Ohara snap-aimed and fired. The two *Nihon-jin* thugs plunged overboard in a death dive.

Keio prepared to reload his M-16 when two more Red Cell men armed with stevedore hooks attacked his position. The Japanese Phoenix Force member raised his empty assault rifle in both hands and blocked a steel hook aimed at his head. He quickly snap-kicked his opponent in the groin and followed up with a butt stroke to the face. Keio hit the JRC hood with such force it shattered the plastic stock of his M-16.

The first terrorist fell, but his comrade took his place. A murderous hook slash narrowly missed Keio as he ducked. The hook whistled overhead and Keio drew his *wakazashi*, pivoting on one knee to add momentum to the sword stroke.

Razor-sharp steel sliced through the terrorist's body, cutting him open with an *ichi-no-do* stroke. The hardguy dropped his hook and fell to the plank walk, his life spilling out in crimson gore.

RAFAEL ENCIZO AND GARY MANNING had been just as busy inside the Hoshiro Company building. Several Japanese Red Cell scum had poured into the storage area from rooms that served as billets for the terrorists. A savage gun battle soon erupted.

Rafael chopped down three terrorists with 9mm lead before they could fire a single shot. Manning opened up on two Nippon-bred mistakes who tried to creep down the stairs to get the drop on Phoenix Force. Slugs sizzled through their chests and pulverized their black hearts. Two more terrorists died, their lifeless bodies tumbling down the stairs.

Rafael charged deeper into the storage room, dodging from one pile of crates to another. A Japanese girl with long black hair and fierce dark eyes suddenly bolted around the corner of the stack of wooden boxes Rafael had chosen for cover. The Cuban ripped apart her face with a trio of 9mm rounds from his MP-5. The girl's hair fanned out as the back of her head exploded, spraying blood and brains on the nearest wall.

"Damn," Encizo groaned.

Manning headed for the stairwell when a stack of crates suddenly crashed down on him.

Two grinning JRC youths eagerly approached the fallen warrior. The terrorists were pleased with their strategy, which had allowed them to attack a formidable opponent without exposing themselves to danger. One junior barbarian kicked Manning's H&K SG1 out of reach while his comrade prepared to finish off the Canadian with a .25 automatic.

The eight-inch barrel of a huge revolver rose from between two crates. The minicannon roared, and a Magnum slug smashed through the center of the young terrorist's chest. The impact hurled the boy's corpse five feet—it slammed into a wall and slid to the floor, smearing blood every inch of the way.

The other kid turned to see Manning sit up, his Smith & Wesson Model 57 held in a two-handed weaver's grip.

"Ee-ya," the boy shouted, but as he cried no, he tried to bring his Skorpion machine pistol into play.

Manning's Magnum bellowed again, and a big semijacketed wadcutter round performed messy brain surgery on the youth's skull. The powerful Canadian climbed to his feet and brushed himself off.

Manning mounted the stairs, his S&W held ready. A terrorist stepped from the cover of a stack of boxes to aim a T50 submachine gun at Manning's broad back.

Rafael, watching for such treachery, fired his MP-5 before the guncock could trigger his North Korean subgun. Four slugs snapped the terrorist's backbone in three places. The would-be assassin did a swift and final nose dive to the floor, dead.

A Red Cell gunman at the head of the stairs jacked a round into a World War II Tokarev pistol—Mother Russia's contribution to the list of worse-made handguns in history. He tried to aim the Soviet junk gun at Manning, but the roar of the .41 Magnum drove him back behind a flight of stairs.

Gary Manning aimed his big Magnum at the enemy's position and waited.

The gunman finally dared to peek around the corner of the stairs, exposing as little of his head as possible. But it was enough for Manning and his

Magnum. The hand-held howitzer erupted, and a .41 slug hit the terrorist under the left eyebrow, punched through skull bone and blew off the top of the man's head.

Manning mounted the stairs and located Hoshiro's office. The room was well lighted and the door featured a large window. He had no problem seeing what Hoshiro Satsu was doing—the portly JRC commander was stuffing file folders into a metal trash can. A can of lighter fluid on the corner of his desk suggested what he planned to do with the records.

Manning slammed a boot into the door, shattering the lock and kicking the door open. Hoshiro stared into the muzzle of the Canadian's Magnum.

"Yamete!" Manning ordered, using one of the few words in his limited Japanese vocabulary.

But Hoshiro did not halt. He defiantly spit at Manning and reached for the lighter fluid. Manning wanted the man alive for interrogation, so he fired the .41, purposely aiming high, blasting a hole through the wall behind Hoshiro.

Hoshiro hardly flinched in response. He threw the can of fluid at Manning before clawing at a small pistol in a pancake holster at the small of his back. Manning again squeezed the trigger of his Magnum. A fat 200-grain slug propelled Hoshiro Satsu backward into a wall. Slowly he dropped, his lifeless body falling to the floor.

Manning walked to the trash can and gazed down at the files. Since the material was written in Japanese, there was no point in trying to read it. He opened the cylinder of his Magnum and dumped out the spent cartridge casings. Manning reached into a pocket for a speedloader with six fresh shells for the revolver.

A massive figure appeared in the doorway.

The Canadian stared at the bulk of Tado as the sumo wrestler stomped into the room. A thin smile crept across Tado's face. His thick fingers flexed, eager for battle.

Gary Manning reluctantly nodded in reply.

11

The sumo wrestler lumbered forward, a rhinoceros in human form. Manning had no intention of trying to fight Tado on his terms. The Canadian closed the cylinder of his empty revolver, grabbed the gun by the barrel and attacked.

Manning feinted with the Magnum as if he planned to use it as a club, then he slammed his left fist into the side of the sumo's head. He quickly rammed the butt of the revolver into the brute's belly and threw another left hook at Tado's skull.

The sumo blocked the second punch. Manning hit him in the solar plexus with the Magnum, but Tado's hand quickly snaked out and snared Manning by the back of the head. Tado pivoted, hurling the Canadian across the room. Manning fell onto the desk and toppled over it, landing unceremoniously on the floor.

He scrambled to his feet, shaking his head to clear the fog. Tado stood in the center of the room, still smiling, apparently unaffected by the punishing blows he had been dealt.

"I'm just warming up, fat boy," Manning growled as he advanced again.

The Canadian feinted with the empty revolver and kicked Tado between the legs as hard as he could. The sumo only grunted in response. Manning swung the Magnum's butt at Tado's head. The Japanese hulk caught his arm and seized Gary's belt with his other hand. Tado picked up the Phoenix Force man and lifted him overhead.

The sumo threw Manning across the room. He slammed into a wall and fell to the floor hard. Lights exploded inside his head, and a crimson veil floated across his eyes.

Manning's vision cleared in time to see Tado waddle to the filing cabinet. The hefty killer picked up the cabinet, then raised the 280-pound piece of office furniture over his head.

"God," the Canadian exclaimed in dismay.

Quickly Manning leaped away from the wall as Tado hurled the cabinet at him. It crashed into the wall, just missing Manning, cracking plaster on impact.

Manning staggered upright. The revolver had been jarred out of his grasp when Tado threw him the second time. Totally unarmed, he faced the sumo wrestler. Tado charged like a rampaging grizzly, thick muscular arms outstretched.

Manning grabbed one of Tado's arms. He half turned and dropped to one knee, pulling the captive limb hard. Tado's forward momentum was increased, and his balance was thrown off by the Canadian's tactic. Tado plunged across the room and fell face first into a water cooler.

The bottle shattered. When Tado turned to face Manning, his smile had vanished. Water and shards of hard plastic spewed across the floor. Blood dripped from cuts on the sumo's face and hands. Burning fury filled his eyes. Manning gestured at his opponent, inviting him to attack again.

The bellow of rage that filled the room hardly seemed human. Tado charged like an angry bull. Manning sidestepped the wrestler's attack. Clasping his hands together, Manning swung hard and hit Tado behind the right ear.

The sumo wrestler staggered and slashed a wild hand chop. He missed. Manning's doubled fists then crashed into his opponent's jaw. The Oriental hulk stumbled, blood trickling from his mouth. Then he lunged again.

Manning dodged the clumsy charge and chopped his doubled hands into Tado's left kidney. The sumo wrestler groaned and fell against the desk. Manning hit him between the shoulder blades and stamped his boot into the back of Tado's knee. The leg buckled and Tado fell to his knees.

Quickly Manning cupped one hand under the wrestler's jaw and placed the heel of his other palm at the side of the sumo's head. He pushed with all his might. Tado's head was violently twisted and vertebrae in his neck crunched. Manning released his opponent and Tado fell face first on the floor. The huge man lay still. Manning had won the right to live.

The Phoenix Force agent rose unsteadily to his feet and leaned against the desk, breathing hard. He felt as if he had been using his body to block cannon-balls. He located his Magnum, picked it up and reloaded the gun.

"Gary," a voice called through the ringing inside Manning's head.

Manning turned to see Yakov Katzenelenbogen in the doorway. The Canadian managed a weak smile.

"We get all of them?" he asked.

"Yes," the Israeli nodded. "And none of our people were injured—that is, if *you're* all right."

"Oh, yeah," Manning assured him. "I got here in time to stop Hoshiro from burning the files," Manning said. "But I had to stop him hard. Sorry. I know we wanted the guy alive."

"None of the rest of us were able to take any prisoners," Yakov shrugged. "We'd better grab those files and get out of here before the police arrive."

"Yeah," Manning agreed. "Things got a little noisy around here."

IKEDA KEN MET PHOENIX FORCE the following morning at the famous Sanzenin Garden. The area featured miles of manicured grass, stately trees, colorful flowers and a magnificent pagoda-style temple.

The Sanzenin Garden was also an ideal site to discuss matters privately, since visitors came to be with their thoughts, not to pry into the affairs of strangers. Ikeda and the men of Phoenix Force strolled through the serene woods.

"The Hoshiro files contain considerable detail

about the names and locations of Red Cell terrorists scattered throughout Japan,'' Yakov explained. ''Your people may find it most useful, Ikeda-*san*.''

''I doubt that there are many of the JRC left,'' the Kompei chief remarked. ''You killed more than sixty terrorists last night.

''Although I admire you all and respect you very much,'' Ikeda sighed, ''I rather hope you will be leaving Nippon soon. Keeping security about your activities here is becoming difficult.''

''We have to complete our mission,'' Manning stated. ''We still haven't located the JRC main headquarters or learned how they've extracted top-secret information from their kidnap victims.''

''We do have a solid lead,'' Yakov added. ''Keio read the files last night and discovered reference to a hydroplane that has made regular trips to the Hoshiro harbor as well as other sites occupied by JRC terrorists.''

''The plane appears to commute from Minami Tori Shima,'' Ohara added.

''An island located in the Tropic of Cancer,'' Ikeda nodded. ''It is property of Japan. I'm familiar with it, my friends. Frankly, I would say it is a most unlikely site for a terrorist headquarters.''

''We agree on that,'' Yakov assured him. ''Such a small island would never do for a terrorist base. Everybody tends to know everybody else, and too many people would be suspicious of a JRC cover operation there. However, it could serve as a go-between for the terrorists in Japan and . . . well, wherever their main headquarters is.''

"Then you think it's somewhere outside the country?" Ikeda asked.

"Too many flights have been going to and from Minami Tori Shima," Keio said. "Passengers, equipment, financial support for the JRC, have all come from there. That suggests the headquarters is *not* in Japan.''

"Then where is it?" the Kompei chief wondered. "North Korea? The Soviet Union?"

"Both Korea and the USSR are a hell of a lot closer than Minami Tori Shima," Rafael said.

"The Communists have supplied the JRC with arms," McCarter said. "And there's probably some sort of connection, but I don't think the Soviets are behind this. Somebody has been financing the terrorists, sending them diamonds—a form of international currency difficult to trace unless the bastards are stupid enough to use large well-known stones. The Russians seldom supply much financial aid to terrorists. Why should they? Most terrorists raise their own support by robbing banks and ransoming hostages.''

The high-pitched whistle of a wooden flute drew their attention to a strange figure that emerged from the tree line. Clad in a dark blue kimono with a yellow *obi* around his waist, the man had a basket made of woven rice reeds covering his head. He held the flute inserted under the rim of the basket as he played it.

"What the hell is that?" Encizo asked.

"He's a *komuso*," Ikeda explained. "A type of itinerant priest. The *komuso* are a tradition in Japan. They wander about playing their *shakuhachi*—bamboo flutes. It is not uncommon to see them here."

"I hope that's what he is," Manning commented. "I don't like having somebody hanging around with his face covered like that."

"He doesn't appear to be armed," Katz noted.

"And he's too far away to hear us," Ohara added. "Even if he had a set of amplifier earphones under the basket, he'd have to use a long-range microphone as well. The *shakuhachi* doesn't conceal one because it wouldn't be functional as a flute."

"You people are going to become paranoid if you continue looking at life in this manner," Ikeda warned.

"Better paranoid than dead," McCarter said. "That's our problem. Let's just concern ourselves with the JRC for now."

"Very well," Ikeda agreed. "If the Russians aren't responsible, who is?"

"Unfortunately," the Israeli said with a sigh, "we don't have the answer yet. Maybe we'll find it at Minami Tori Shima."

"The Pacific Ocean surrounding the island is peppered with other island nations," Encizo stated. "Like the Philippines. I think we can safely say that the Philippine government wouldn't assist the JRC."

"The Moro Liberation Front and the New People's Army," Gary Manning began, referring to the major terrorist organizations active in the Philippines, "couldn't be behind anything this big either."

"And Japanese terrorists couldn't operate on their own in the Philippines," Ohara added. "Filipinos and our people have never gotten along very well."

"True," Ikeda agreed. "It seems we know where the terrorists *can't* be but still have no idea where they are."

"By process of elimination," McCarter said, "we're bound to figure out where to look."

A large group of Buddhist monks appeared from the direction of the temple. They wore saffron robes and bowed their shaven heads low as they shuffled forward. The monks chanted softly, their shoulders moving with the rhythm of their song.

When the monks had passed, Ikeda picked up the conversation. "Unfortunately," Ikeda said grimly, "our situation has become even more desperate. Aaron Palmer was abducted last night."

"Palmer?" The Canadian frowned. "Isn't he the deputy director of the Central Intelligence Agency?"

Ikeda nodded. "Palmer arrived at Tokyo International Airport. Kompei and the police took every precaution, but the terrorists still kidnapped him."

The Kompei chief explained what he knew about the Palmer abduction. Phoenix Force listened, fully appreciating the critical nature of the CIA official's kidnapping. Gary Manning shook his head.

"Any idea how the bastards knew about Palmer?" the Canadian asked.

"His visit here was not . secret," Ikeda replied.

"Virtually anyone could have known about it in advance."

"The United States had better get a National Secrets Act," McCarter muttered. "Their security has gone to hell in a hand basket."

"The terrorists probably assumed Palmer would be moved from Tokyo," Katz commented. "They probably ambushed and killed some policemen in order to get their uniforms and cars. Then they simply mingled with the other cops and waited."

"They could have kept in touch by walkie-talkie," Ohara added. "When they found the Migato hotel was blocked off by the police, they knew where to plan the hit on Palmer's group."

"Then they sacrificed one of their own," Encizo said. "The sniper got to die for the cause. Naturally the cops rushed Palmer into the shelter of the hotel and right into the arms of the Red Cell."

"Hell," Manning said with a sigh, "with that sort of strategy, the terrorists don't have to use a brain-draining device."

"They'll need it to get information out of Palmer," the Israeli stated. "I know Aaron. He's tough, and he's received every type of counter-interrogation training possible."

"None of which will stop the JRC from plucking his mind like a fig tree," McCarter commented, but his eyes were fixed on the *komuso* priest.

The man had stopped playing his flute and slid the *shakuhachi* into a slit in his kimono. McCarter did not like the *komuso*'s behavior. The priest had not done anything suspicious, but the Briton's sixth sense was screaming a red alert inside his head.

"We can only guess how many vital secrets the terrorists will learn from Palmer," Ohara said grimly. He also watched the *komuso* like a hawk and saw the man produce another bamboo flute from his robe.

"Too many," Manning remarked. "We've got to find the Red Cell headquarters and Palmer within twenty-four hours or national security for the United States of America goes right in the toilet."

"We'll have to stay alive long enough to do it," Encizo added, jerking his head at the advancing congregation of Buddhist monks.

"What do you mean?" Ikeda inquired.

"It looks like the tranquillity of this garden is about to be disturbed," Katz replied sadly.

The *komuso* tilted the basket up to his forehead as he raised the new flute to his lips and aimed it at Ikeda Ken. Ohara quickly lunged forward and grabbed the Kompei man by the shoulders. He pulled Ikeda aside and pushed him to the ground as he raised the briefcase in his fist.

The *shakuhachi* was actually a solid bamboo tube with a mouthpiece attached to the end the "priest" blew into. Something hissed from the muzzle of the man's blowgun. The projectile struck Ohara's case, the steel dart burying its point in the lid.

McCarter was the first to draw his weapon from leather. He aimed the Browning Hi-Power autoloader and squeezed the trigger. A jagged bullet hole appeared in the rice-reed basket three inches above the bamboo blowgun still in the assassin's mouth. The "*kosumo*" dropped his flute, and the basket fell back into position over his bullet-punctured head an instant before his corpse toppled to the ground.

Shouting a battle cry, the eleven "monks" attacked. They pulled fighting knives from the sleeves of their robes, which concealed the sheaths strapped to their forearms.

McCarter fired into the advancing group. One of the monks fell, clutching his chest. The others kept coming. One of the assailants suddenly leaped forward like a panther and dived into the Briton. Both men tumbled backward into the stream.

"Damn it," Gary Manning snorted as he tried to draw his .41 Magnum S&W revolver.

The long-barreled handgun was not designed for a fast draw. Manning was a second too late. A knife-wielding terrorist slashed at his throat before the Canadian could clear leather. Manning narrowly dodged the blade and nearly tripped over Ikeda who was scrambling across the ground, trying to get back on his feet.

The utter boldness of the killers proved to be their greatest ally. Their lunatic charge had caught Phoenix Force off guard and allowed them to close in before most of the defenders could bring a weapon into play.

Keio Ohara's pistol was in his briefcase. The tall Japanese warrior did not bother trying to get to it. He dropped the luggage and turned to face one of the knife-wielding attackers.

Ohara feinted a kick at the "monk's" groin. The terrorist slashed his knife at Ohara's ankle and missed when Keio cut the kick short. Ohara rapidly swung his other leg in a roundhouse kick to the killer's elbow that struck the ulna nerve and jarred his arm, forcing the man to drop his knife.

Ohara shot a *seiken* punch to his opponent's face. The terrorist staggered two steps backward as Ohara turned and drove a left-legged side kick into the man's midsection. He immediately followed up with a wheel kick, whirling like a top, lashing his right leg in a high arch. The back of his heel crashed into the side of his opponent's skull, caving in the man's sphenoid bone.

Gary Manning avoided a knife thrust and caught his opponent's wrist before the killer could draw back his arm. The Canadian's other hand grabbed the thug's neck as he jerked the man forward. The terrorist was off balance as Manning quickly twisted his arm in a hammerlock and forced the assailant to drive his own knife into his lower back.

The assassin screamed as sharp steel punctured his right kidney. Manning used the wounded man as a shield and pulled him in front of a second knife artist who had just launched an attack. The second terrorist gasped when he accidentally stabbed his comrade in the stomach.

The Canadian used the wounded man for a battering ram and shoved him into the second assailant. Both terrorists fell to the ground with Manning on top of them. The powerful Canadian seized each man by the hair and smashed their heads together with skull-crushing force.

Ikeda Ken managed to get to one knee and drew his Nambu pistol, only to have it kicked out of his hand by another assassin. The killer held his knife in an overhand grip and prepared to drive the blade into his intended victim.

Fear contributed to Ikeda's speed as he quickly braced himself on both hands and punted a foot into the terrorist's kneecap. The assassin stumbled and awkwardly struck out with his knife.

The Kompei chief rolled out of the path of the blade, and the killer drove his weapon into the ground where Ikeda had been a split second before. Pivoting on the small of his back, Ikeda shifted into position and slammed a foot into his assailant's face. Blood squirted from the man's pulverized nose as he flopped over on his back. Ikeda quickly uprooted the knife from the ground and buried the blade in his opponent's chest.

Colonel Yakov Katzenelenbogen blocked a knife with his right forearm. The blade snapped in two when it struck the steel prosthetic arm. Before the terrorist could recover from his astonishment, Katz drew his .45 Colt Commander and backhanded the pistol across his opponent's face.

The assassin fell. Katz thumbed off the safety catch of his pistol and shot the terrorist in his shaven head. Suddenly a pair of hands seized the Israeli's wrist and twisted the .45 from Katz's grasp.

Another hoodlum had lost his knife in the scuffle

and saw a chance to get a pistol by disarming the Israeli, who appeared to be the oldest and weakest member of Phoenix Force. The man soon realized he had underestimated Katz when the Israeli colonel stamped a hard mule kick into the side of his knee.

The man's leg buckled from the kick. Katzenelenbogen turned sharply and slashed his prosthetic hand at his adversary's face. The points of the steel hooks ripped through flesh and tore an eyeball from its socket. The terrorist screamed and clamped both hands over his bloodied face.

Katz chopped the side of his left hand into the man's solar plexus. With a moan, the killer doubled up. The Israeli swung his hook again and smashed it into the base of his foe's skull. The would-be assassin fell forward to receive a knee in the face. Katz had not needed to deliver the last stroke—his opponent was already dead.

Rafael Encizo sidestepped a knife thrust and deftly kicked his attacker in the testicles. The terrorist gasped and fell to his knees. Encizo quickly drew his Gerber Mark I from its sheath as another shaven-headed goon charged forward, slashing at the Cuban's throat with a knife.

Encizo dodged the whistling blade and struck with the speed and accuracy of a cobra. His Gerber knife slashed the other man's wrist before he could pull his arm away. Blood spurted from severed arteries as the terrorist shrieked and dropped his weapon.

The Cuban quickly lunged into his wounded opponent and drove the point of his Gerber into the terrorist's solar plexus, stabbing the steel tip upward into the man's heart. Encizo yanked the knife from the mortally wounded guy and shoved his dying opponent aside.

Two more knife-wielding assailants attacked.

Encizo moved to the right to avoid being trapped between the two men and narrowly leaped away from a blade that was lashed at one man's belly. He quickly switched the Gerber from his right hand to his left and struck out at his nearest opponent.

It was an old knife fighter's trick to try to hit an adversary from an unexpected direction. Most Hispanic knife artists are familiar with this technique, but it worked well enough against the terrorist. The Cuban's Gerber slashed a deep furrow in his opponent's forearm.

The terrorist cried out and withdrew his arm, the saffron sleeve of his robe dyed red with blood. Encizo promptly punched the man in the mouth and knocked him backward into the other enemy knife artist.

"Enough of this," the Cuban muttered as he drew his Walther PPK and thumbed off the safety catch.

The compact double-action pistol snarled as Encizo squeezed the trigger. He fired three rapid-fire rounds into the horrified faces of the two terrorists. The first man took a hollowpoint slug in the forehead and dropped dead instantly.

His partner caught a bullet in the left cheek. It splintered bone and cracked his eye socket. He was already in shock when the second .380 shattered the bone of his upper jaw and tunneled into his brain.

David McCarter had found himself thrashing in the stream with an opponent, but he ended the wrestling match abruptly by slamming the steel frame of his Browning against the other man's skull. Then he turned the terrorist on his belly in the creek and simply sat on the man's back, holding the killer's face in the water until he was certain the thug had drowned.

"Damnation on Easter Sunday," the Briton complained as he stepped from the creek, dripping wet from head to toe. "That son of a bitch ruined this suit."

"Isn't it wash and wear?" Ohara asked with a grin.

He noticed the only survivor of the enemy forces was still on his knees, clutching his genitals. Ohara quickly stepped behind the thug and clapped his open palms against the man's ears. The concussion ruptured both eardrums and sent a brain-jarring shock through the hoodlum's skull. The man fell on his face, unconscious.

"Wring out your jacket, McCarter," Katz urged as he shoved his Colt Commander into shoulder leather. "We'd better get out of here *fast*."

"I thought I recognized this man," Ikeda Ken declared as he knelt beside the assailant he had killed during the battle.

"Someone important?" Encizo asked.

"Yakuza," the Kompei chief replied. "A member of the *Isimoto Obyan*. A small-time criminal outfit. They're mostly strong-arm bullies, hired to handle the less delicate matters that the larger Yakuza clans would refuse to touch.''

"That explains why they didn't use guns," Keio Ohara added. "Yakuza don't favor firearms. They don't feel they need guns since very few Japanese own firearms."

"Except the terrorists," McCarter said dryly.

"At least this will make a cover story for this incident—make it easy to fabricate," Ikeda stated. "Yakuza killing Yakuza doesn't get anyone very excited. Least of all the police who are simply thankful no innocent people were harmed and some undesirable criminals are no longer a threat."

"But why would the Red Cell hire gangsters to try to kill us?" Manning wondered.

"Because their own manpower must be dwindling," Encizo replied. "The Japanese Red Cell must be dying off—literally."

"Here in Japan, perhaps," Katzenelenbogen said. "But we've only hacked off a few tentacles of the terrorist octopus. We've still got to find the head and destroy it."

12

"We need transportation to Hawaii," Yakov Katzenelenbogen declared. "Fast."

"Hawaii?" Hal Brognola questioned, speaking into the handset of an international transceiver in the control center of Stony Man headquarters.

"Our business investigation has led to a firm in Hawaii," the Israeli answered. "We hope to have a final conference there."

Brognola smiled. Stony Man received transmissions via a special communications satellite equipped with a scrambler. Still, Yakov, a total professional, remained security conscious and never discussed the details of a mission in direct terms.

"A representative from one of our associate businesses seems to be in trouble," Brognola said, referring to Aaron Palmer.

"We're aware of that," Yakov assured him. "If we can locate him, we'll try to assist."

"I'm sure you'll do what you can," the Fed replied.

"We'll also need whatever information you can give us about the president of the Hawaiian firm...." Yakov hesitated, not wanting to give a name directly in transmission, yet unable to code it in a manner that would not cause a delay in translation. "A Mr. Edward Oshimi."

Phoenix Force had learned about Oshimi when they had checked the flight records at an airstrip in Minami Tori Shima. The hydroplane that traveled back and forth for the JRC was registered to Edward Oshimi at Honolulu International Airport. So was a twin-engine Cessna that had departed the island to return to Hawaii, only a few hours after the Palmer kidnapping.

"Oshimi," Brognola confirmed, well aware that the matter must be critical for Yakov to speak bluntly. "I'll look into it. Get back to you soon."

"That'll be fine, sir," Yakov said.

"Let me get the address of a travel agent associated with our firm."

"I'll hold," the Israeli replied.

Brognola left the transceiver and told Stony Man computer expert, Aaron Kurtzman, that Phoenix Force needed a fast secure method of transportation from Japan to Hawaii. "The Bear" quickly consulted one of the Stony Man computers.

Kurtzman fed the data via a keyboard console. Seconds later numbers and names appeared on the video-display screen. Kurtzman hit the print button and a readout sheet emerged from a word processor hooked up to the computer.

Two minutes later Brognola had the transceiver handset in his fist. "Still there?"

"Yes, sir," Yakov assured him.

"Okay," the Fed began. "Go to 20th Street and find travel agent's office at number 170. His name is C. Burke, a retired Navy officer."

"Got it," the Israeli confirmed.

"Good luck," Brognola said.

"We'll need it," Yakov admitted. "Thank you."

End of transmission.

Katzenelenbogen read the address of the "travel agent." He deciphered 20th Street as twenty degrees latitude and number 170 to be the longitude coordinates. Consulting a map, he found the location in the Pacific. Brognola's coordinates were not exact, but they were close to Wake Island.

C. Burke—Commander Burke. Retired Navy? A little white lie. The commander was probably an officer in the ONI stationed at the naval base in Wake Island. By the time Phoenix Force arrived, Burke would have a plane ready to take them to Hawaii.

"Do a complete personal profile on Edward Oshimi," Hal Brognola said as he turned to Kurtzman. "Probable residence in the Hawaiian Islands. Sounds like he's a U.S. citizen, but be ready to check immigration just in case. If you don't get anything there, get in touch with the Treasury Department—which is also the National Central Bureau of the American branch of Interpol."

"Right, Hal," he nodded.

"I want everything available on this Oshimi character," Brognola continued. "Personal background, politics, former military service, government security clearances, criminal record—anything. Especially if it relates to Japan or terrorism. If the name is an alias, I want to know who he really is.''

''I'll get that for you, Hal,'' Kurtzman said, his fingers already punching the computer console. *''Fast,''* he added, chomping on the stem of his pipe.

AARON PALMER AWOKE to find himself dressed in silk pajamas, lying on a comfortable sofa, his head resting on a soft pillow. Music played gently in the background. Palmer was not certain what the tune was, but the melody was pretty, played on violins, soft piano and a harp.

The CIA man gazed up at the ceiling. It was painted a soft shade of pink. He heard an air conditioner humming gently. *Where the hell am I,* Palmer thought. Then he wondered why it had taken him so long to feel concern about the fact that he did not know where he was or how he had gotten there.

He was not home or at his office, and the place did not seem to be a hotel room. Palmer gradually turned his head to inspect his quarters. He was surprised to discover he felt weak and weary. Yet Palmer was not alarmed until he saw the steel bars on the room's only door.

''Jesus,'' he whispered hoarsely. ''I'm in a goddamn cell.''

Only then did the memories of the kidnapping return to him. Even then, he was not certain that it had not been a dream. It did not seem possible that he could feel so relaxed after being abducted. Yet he experienced a total sense of well-being and pleasant exhaustion.

"This is real," he told himself. "This is a prison cell."

Palmer rolled over the edge of the sofa and fell to the carpeted floor, trying to jar the reality of the situation into his dazed foggy mind. *The bastards drugged me,* he thought. *Scopolamine will be next . . . or torture.*

The deputy director of the CIA tried to prepare himself for whatever ordeal awaited him. Drugs would not be a problem, not even the GB/Sarin compound. Hypnosis would not work, either, because Palmer knew how it worked and how to guard against subtle hypnotic suggestion.

Torture was another matter. Some people claim to be masters of astral projection. That might be the ideal method of dealing with torture—by sending one's soul out of the body while the bad guys oil their thumbscrews. But Palmer did not believe in Eastern mysticism and even if it worked, the astral body would still have to come back to a butchered shell afterward.

There are only two practical ways to deal with torture. One is suicide. The other is to tell your captors convincing lies and half truths and hope they buy it.

Professional torturers take their time with a subject. Psychology is as much a tool as actual pain. They will let a victim's mind prey on the various types of horror that man can inflict on a fellow human being and hope the subject will frighten himself into breaking.

The torturers would not do anything that might cause heart failure or shock...not at first, anyway. They would probably start with the feet and hands because thousands of nerve endings are located there and half the two hundred six bones in a human body are in these extremities. They would not graduate to eyeball gouging and castration until later.

Palmer would have to endure as much torment as possible before he started to blab misleading and false information to his keepers. He would have to make it convincing and not spill too much too quickly. It would be the most ugly, horrible experience in his life. Palmer trembled.

"Where are those poison capsules I read about in the spy novels," he muttered out loud.

"If you had had one we would have found it and confiscated it," a voice declared.

Palmer gazed up at a heavyset man with Asian features who stood at the barred door. He wore a black Oriental robe of some sort, and a pair of uniformed muscle boys stood in the corridor beside him.

"Don't tell me," Palmer began, trying to sound calmer than he felt. "You studied English at UCLA, right? Go back home, fella. I'm not going to tell you shit."

"You will tell us everything we want to know, Palmer," Oshimi replied. "And you won't have to say a word."

Aaron Palmer stared at his jailer. *The guy's bluff-*

ing, he thought, trying to convince himself that Oshimi's confidence was a facade.

"Okay, Fu Manchu," Palmer sneered. "Let's get on with it, you bastard."

"My feelings exactly," Oshimi smiled.

13

The F-4 Phantom fighter jet landed at the U.S. Naval Base at Pearl Harbor on the Hawaiian island of Oahu. Commander Burke had personally flown Phoenix Force to their destination. He did not ask any questions about their mission. ONI had told him the five men had a top-level clearance from the Oval Office.

Of course, Burke had wondered about his passengers and their luggage. He had noticed that three of the men packed guns under their jackets. The Hispanic and the Oriental were probably heeled, too, but Burke had not noticed the telltale bulges of concealed weapons. The Japanese had some sort of sword in a cloth case, and the commander could only guess how much hardware they had in their baggage—or what they would do with it when they reached Hawaii.

Burke watched the mystery men walk from the plane. He should have been offended. After all, he was a commander in the United States Navy, and he had been reduced to the level of an airborne taxi driver. Yet, somehow he felt there was no disgrace in assisting these five men.

A tall lean man with iron-gray hair, dressed in a

white uniform and carrying an attaché case, met
Phoenix Force at the runway. His shoulder boards
held the rank of rear admiral, and the sour expression on his face revealed he was less than delighted to
meet the five men.

"I'm Admiral St. Clair," he announced stiffly.
"I've been instructed by Fleet Admiral Sirak to assist
you in any way possible."

"We appreciate your situation," Katzenelenbogen
said quickly. "This is certainly awkward for you, but
I hope you understand this is a very important matter
of national security."

"I realize that," St. Clair replied. "But I'm not
accustomed to taking orders from civilians."

"We're all acting in the interest of the United
States of America," Manning told him.

"So I've been told," St. Clair replied, nodding. He
handed the briefcase to Yakov. "This was delivered
by a special courier. I was told the combination lock
is identical to the 'number of the fish.' I assume you
know what that means."

"I hope so," the Israeli said, grinning. "Hate to
have to shoot the lock off."

St. Clair was not amused. He escorted them to a
U.S. Government limousine. Phoenix Force climbed
into the back; the admiral drove the vehicle. Yakov
then passed the briefcase to Rafael.

One of the Cuban's nicknames was Pescado or
"Fish," given to him because of his ability as a
frogman. The "number of the fish" referred to Encizo's social-security number. Rafael worked the

combination and opened the briefcase. Inside the
valise were five file folders, one for each member of
Phoenix Force.

The information inside the folders was identical. It
concerned an individual: Professor Edward Oshimi.

EDWARD OSHIMI was fifty-three years old. Japanese
American. He and his family had been moved to
an internment camp during World War II because
of U.S. government concern about possible espionage agents among Asian Americans. While in
confinement, Edward's mother had died of tuber-
culosis.

After the war Hirito Oshimi, Edward's father,
made a remarkable climb. He became the manager
of a Japanese-American corporation that imported
transistorized products from Japan. This proved
highly profitable in the 1950s.

Edward, meanwhile, excelled in school. A genius
in mathematics and physics, he enrolled in the
Cheney College of Advanced Sciences and continued
to earn scholastic honors.

In 1956 the senior Oshimi died of stomach cancer.
Because of his success as a businessman and his
wisdom in careful investments and savings, he left
$12,000,000 to Edward, his only son.

Only twenty-seven years old, wealthy, brilliant,
working as a physicist for the government's Department of Defense Research Office, Edward Oshimi
had a golden future. He became a strong voice for
cooperation between the U.S. and Japan and made

frequent trips to the Orient, meeting with fellow scientists to try and achieve this cooperation.

During one of his visits, Oshimi married Mikko Hotashi. Her father, Kakuei Hotashi, had been a lieutenant in the Japanese Imperial Navy during the war. Kakuei was descended from a family of samurai warriors and had been training as a kamikaze pilot when the emperor surrendered.

Kakuei Hotashi held total contempt for Americans and Western culture, which he considered to be a cancer that threatened to ruin Nippon. The marriage of his daughter to an American, even one of Japanese descent, should have outraged Hotashi. However, he seemed quite pleased with Mikko's choice. The reason for this would later be a matter of concern for the United States—Oshimi was loyal to Japan, not the Japan of the present but the empire that had been defeated when it charged into the twentieth century too quickly.

Oshimi hated America. He regarded it as the country that had imprisoned his family and killed his mother. He gave credit to Japan, not the U.S., for his father's success and his own wealth. Edward Oshimi was as militant as Kakuei.

A year after their marriage, Mikko was killed in a car accident. Oshimi took her body back to Japan for burial. Hotashi attended the funeral, then returned home alone. That night he committed *seppuku*, the ancient ritual of suicide by disemboweling oneself with a knife or short sword.

Oshimi returned to the United States and worked

as a research scientist for the Defense Department's experiments with lasers in the early 1960s. He excelled in this field, but never received a promotion to a high security level because his loyalty to the U.S., as well as his emotional stability, were questionable. Oshimi considered his lack of advancement to be racial discrimination by the nation he had grown to despise.

Oshimi continued to work on innovations on the laser until 1973 when he presented a proposal to the Pentagon. Oshimi claimed to have perfected a laser weapon that could fire a concentrated beam of light capable of piercing the armor of a T-60 Russian tank from a distance of five hundred miles.

However, Oshimi insisted on certain conditions before he would turn over his patent to the government. The weapon would have to be manufactured as a combined effort by the United States and Japan. The Japanese defensive military forces would be altered to become stronger, according to the terms of Oshimi's demands—and half the new laser cannons would be promised to Nippon.

American involvement in Vietnam was coming to an end, and the government was not eager to build up military strength in the Orient after finally bringing the U.S. out of the controversial conflict. Besides, other inventors were working on laser weapons, and plans for "killer satellites" were already in progress. The Pentagon rejected Oshimi's proposal.

Enraged by this refusal, Professor Edward Oshimi resigned from his government job. Until 1976 he worked as a technical advisor for a corporation in San Diego that specialized in the development of industrial lasers. Then, Oshimi retired at the age of forty-five and moved to Hawaii.

The FBI and the Justice Department kept Oshimi under surveillance for a short time. It seemed highly unlikely that a multimillionaire capitalist would defect to the Soviet Union or China. Far more likely was the possibility Oshimi might attempt to sell information to the Japanese government, although he had never been trusted with any state secrets unknown to America's allies.

The Feds were more concerned that enemy agents might con the bitter professor out of his fortune than any secret-weapon pipe dreams Oshimi might conjure up. Since the Oshimi nest egg had continued to grow to almost $25,000,000, it had become large enough to attract the KGB or the Chinese SAD, either of which would be happy to acquire such a windfall for the coffers at Moscow or Peking.

Surveillance teams were surprised to discover Oshimi had purchased a coffee plantation along the Kona Coast, one of the few privately owned plantations in the only region of the United States that grows coffee. The biggest shock was the fact Oshimi had ordered the construction of a fortress—a pagoda-style structure similar to the fabled Osaka Castle.

This was considered highly eccentric but not out of character for Edward Oshimi. No one was surprised that he sold most of his coffee to Japan or that his staff consisted exclusively of Japanese and Japanese Americans. The government decided to leave Oshimi alone and allow him to play make-believe *daimyo*.

Although the Feds lost interest in Oshimi, several Hawaiian police departments were concerned when they learned many of the professor's employees had criminal records. Twice investigations of Oshimi's plantation were conducted. The first was a simple head count of ex-cons on Oshimi's payroll. The second was to check out a report that the plantation was patrolled by sentries armed with machine guns. However, the weapons proved to be civilian model CAR-15 semiautomatic rifles. None of the guard force had criminal records, and Oshimi assured the cops that the former jailbirds worked in the fields and never touched a firearm.

Money talks, and Oshimi used it to scream at the state legislation. Accusations of police harassment forced the Hawaiian police to back off from the plantation.

The only other official information about Oshimi concerned his Cessna airplanes at the Keahole and Honolulu airports. Aircraft flew from Hawaii to Oahu and from Oahu to Japan. The flights were listed as "business," and no one had any reason to suspect otherwise—until now.

The photographs from the U.S. files consisted of several pictures of Edward Oshimi. As a young man Oshimi had been muscular with a lean hard face and fierce eyes. The most recent photo was of a middle-aged man with a double chin, a full face and a shaven head. Only the bitterness of his mouth and the hostility in his eyes remained.

There was also a photo of his castle. Orchards of small trees with leaves that appeared to be made of wet plastic surrounded a stone wall that circled the building. The castle was unbelievable, a fortress of stone and mortar and tile. Stacked four stories high, it had gracefully sloped roofs with curved eaves extending from each segment. Every window featured thick shutters.

In startling contrast, a white dome sat at the summit of the castle. A long telescope extended from the center of the observatory.

"There's our target," David McCarter declared, jabbing a finger at his copy of the castle photo.

"We don't know that," Gary Manning warned.

"Bullshit," Rafael Encizo snorted. "Do you think this is all coincidence?"

"Wait a minute," Manning insisted. "I've never questioned anything we've done before, but we've always been one hundred percent certain about a target in the past. We're only about eighty percent sure this time."

"That's the key word, Gary," Keio said. "*Time*. We're running out of it fast."

"Keio's right," Yakov agreed. "The terrorists have had Aaron Palmer long enough to pump his brain dry. Oshimi Castle *has* to be right."

"Let's do it," Manning muttered.

14

The Bell UH-1D helicopter flew through the dark night sky. It hovered over the island of Molokai, once known as The Lonely Island; the Kalaupapa Peninsula had housed the infamous leper colony where Father Damien de Veuster became a martyr. Modern-day Molokai is not lonely or depressing—it is a tourist paradise with beaches, forests, parks and picnic grounds.

The helicopter passed over Molokai and flew over Lanai, the smallest of the six major Hawaiian islands. The chopper continued over Maui, the second most popular island.

At last, the helicopter approached its destination—the island of Hawaii, the largest of the isles with over four thousand square miles of land. To the east of Hawaii is the tropical region of Hilo, the greatest orchid center in the world. It is the home base for the largest privately owned cattle ranch on the face of the earth and the awesome Mauna Loa, the biggest active volcano in the world.

David McCarter piloted the Bell UH-1D as it hovered along the Alenuihaha Channel. The Kohala Peninsula, which is the birthplace of Kamehameha, the legendary warrior-king, is located here. Some call him the George Washington of Hawaii, others cast him in the role of a selfish opportunist who betrayed his people to the Western powers. Nonetheless, Kamehameha's statue in Kohala remains one of the island's most popular attractions.

The helicopter moved south to the Kona Coast. McCarter located the Keahole Airport and radioed for permission to land. Minutes later the Bell UH-1D touched down.

"Nice of Admiral St. Clair to let us borrow this chopper, isn't it?" McCarter said with a grin.

"He's got a job to do," Yakov commented as he climbed out of the Bell. "Just like us. The only difference is he acts like a jerk about it."

"I don't think he's acting," Keio added.

"Who cares either way?" Manning asked. "I'll still send him a thank-you card if he keeps supplying us with support."

"And it looks like he is," Yakov stated, gesturing with his prosthetic hand.

The steel hook pointed at a military jeep that was being driven along the runway toward Phoenix Force. Two young men, clad in blue Naval fatigues rode in the vehicle. The members of Phoenix Force nodded with approval when they noticed the sailors wore the blue berets of the SEALS.

The jeep came to a halt and one of the SEALS stepped out of the vehicle. He was tall, lean and muscular with dark brown eyes and a small scar on his left cheek. The man wore no insignia of rank on his collar, but the .45 Colt on his right hip suggested he was a commissioned officer.

"Lieutenant Randisi, reporting, sir," the man declared with a crisp salute.

"Glad to have you on the mission, Lieutenant," Yakov replied, returning the salute with his metal claw.

"Thank you, sir," Randisi said. "This is Chief Petty Officer Murphy." He introduced the driver.

"I understand you're a qualified chopper pilot," McCarter said.

"Yes, sir," Randisi answered. "Both Murphy and I are qualified for gunship duty."

"How many flying hours do you have in a copter?"

"Over eight hundred logged," the lieutenant replied. "Most of that was flying Hueys, and I'm familiar with the UH-1D."

"Very good," the Briton nodded with satisfaction.

Keio Ohara carried a field radio to the jeep. "This transceiver has been modified to receive a special UHF transmission identical to the setting of the radio in this chopper."

"We're taking the jeep," Rafael explained. "You'll stay in touch with us via the radio."

"I understood speed to be vital to this mission," Randisi remarked, wondering why they would not all travel by helicopter.

"It is," Manning confirmed. "But stealth is just as important. It's pretty hard to sneak into a place with a big noisy helicopter."

"We will remain in contact by radio," Yakov said. "You will receive the exact location of the target site of an enemy stronghold."

"The gunship is fully armed with UH-1C rockets and machine guns," Rafael stated.

"In other words," McCarter added, "you'll have more than enough to destroy the target."

"Yes, sir," Randisi said, nodding woodenly.

"Let's synchronize watches," Manning said. "Make it 2100 hours. Less confusion that way."

"Lieutenant Randisi," Yakov began, "when we have completed our mission, you may be contacted and given orders, depending on our needs at that time. If we don't relay a message to you by 0500 hours, you are to attack and *destroy* the stronghold."

"Including you five if you haven't gotten out of there?" Murphy asked.

"We're expendable," Yakov answered.

"Aren't we all," Randisi remarked with a shrug.

RAFAEL ENCIZO DROVE THE JEEP with the other members of Phoenix Force and their equipment crammed into the vehicle. Keio Ohara examined a road map with a flashlight, while Gary Manning scanned the area through infrared Starlite binoculars.

"According to the map," Keio said, "Route 90 South leads to Route 18, which extends through the coffee region of the Kona Coast. So we should be getting closer."

"Finding the right plantation shouldn't be difficult," Yakov said. "How many Japanese castles are likely to be in the area?"

"There'd better be only one," Manning remarked, lowering his Starlite. "And we're heading toward it. About eight kilometers to the east."

Minutes later they arrived at the boundaries of the Oshimi Coffee Plantation. A steel-wire fence surrounded acres of tiny coffee trees. The castle, a large ominous shape in the distance, seemed to lurk in the plantation like a large beast. The headlights of the jeep illuminated a sign mounted on the fence: *Kapu!* Private Property! Keep Out!

"What the hell does *kapu* mean?" McCarter wondered.

"It's Hawaiian," Rafael answered as he pulled over to the side of the road and turned off the engine. "I guess it means the same as the other words in English."

"Maybe we should have worn colorful shirts and flower garlands around our necks," Manning joked, strapping on his field pack full of explosives. "Then we could have claimed we were lost tourists."

"Dressed in camouflage black and packing all these weapons," Rafael said, "we'd be convincing if we said we were looking for *pakalolo*. Marijuana crops are big business in Hawaii, especially here in Kona. Growers often protect their weed with armed guards and trap guns."

"No matter what we told Oshimi's people," Yakov commented, "they'd still shoot us if they had the chance."

Keio contacted Lieutenant Randisi on the radio while the others checked their weapons. The Japanese warrior switched off the transceiver and checked his guns. He had brought an Ingram M-10 machine pistol, better suited for close quarters than his M-16 assault rifle. He had also chosen a Colt 1911A1 instead of his AutoMag because the pistol and Ingram both fired .45-caliber ammunition. The other members of Phoenix carried the same weaponry they had used in Japan.

They checked the fence for alarm wires. Although they did not find any, it was possible a pressure unit under the fence could trigger an alarm if they climbed or cut it. That was a risk they would have to take. There was no time to check everything. Oshimi could have heat sensors, infrared scanners, microwave sensors or a dozen other invisible security devices.

Manning tossed a rock against the fence to see if it was electric. When no sparks appeared, Rafael and Keio attacked the fence with wire cutters. Two minutes later Phoenix Force slipped through the opening and entered Oshimi's plantation.

They moved through the coffee bushes, keeping low, all senses alert to possible danger. A bright half-moon and a riot of stars overhead shone down on the plantation. The night was quiet—too quiet.

Suddenly the rumble of a car grabbed their attention. Phoenix Force ducked behind some coffee bushes as a pair of headlights sliced through the shadows. Peering between leaves and branches, they saw a Toyota Land Cruiser rolling along a dirt road that bisected the field. Two men, clad in khaki bush shirts, rode in the jeep—the driver and a man with a pump shotgun.

"Give them a sore foot," Yakov whispered to McCarter. He turned to Keio and said, "Don't kill unless you have to."

The Land Cruiser continued along the road until McCarter convinced it to stop. The silencer attached to his Ingram rasped, and bullets ripped into the front and rear tires on the driver's side of the jeep. The vehicle weaved violently until the driver stomped on the brake.

Keio broke cover and dashed to the crippled jeep from behind. He caught the spare tire mounted to the rear of the Toyota and used it for a brace as he swung his long body over the top of the open carriage. The shotgunner presented the most serious immediate threat. Keio took him out first with a flying roundhouse kick. The toe of his paratrooper boot caught the startled sentry full in the mouth, breaking several teeth and his jaw.

The shotgun man's unconscious body collided with the driver, who was awkwardly trying to draw a pistol from a belt holster. Keio reached him before he could clear leather. The Japanese warrior's hands struck like axes. He *shuto* chopped the driver's forearm to prevent him from drawing the weapon. Another blow hit the man behind the ear, and a third slammed into the side of his neck. The sentry slumped behind the wheel.

Then white light flooded the captured jeep. Another Land Cruiser had suddenly appeared, rapidly closing the distance, its shotgun man holding his weapon to his shoulder.

Rafael's MP-5 belched softly, and a stream of 9mm rounds burst from the silenced H&K machine pistol. The shotgunner was kicked over the side of the speeding jeep; his bullet-riddled body hit the road and rolled limply into a drainage ditch.

Before the driver could react, Gary Manning had pounced from the bushes. He dived onto the moving jeep, crashing into the stunned sentry. The jeep zigged, zagged and nose-dived into the coffee fields.

Manning clubbed the guard in the face with the bottom of his fist. He hit the guy again in the temple before he seized the steering wheel and applied the brake. The Land Cruiser had run over yards of shrubs and berries, crushing dozens of little trees.

Rafael ran up to Manning, prepared to help; but no help was needed. "The driver of the jeep is dead," Manning said. "Guess I hit him too hard."

"You can't hit a terrorist too hard," Rafael stated.

"But we're not certain the security people for the coffee plantation are terrorists," Keio said. "They might be hirelings unaware of Oshimi's activities."

"So bind the two you rendered unconscious," Yakov told him. "We had to kill the other two. There wasn't any choice. Terrorists, hired help or saints—they were carrying guns and now they're dead. We can't bring them back to life."

15

Keio Ohara used plastic riot cuffs to bind the wrists and ankles of the patrol's survivors. All the guards were Oriental. The man with the broken jaw was not in any condition to talk, so Keio only revived the other guard he had knocked out.

Keio massaged the carotid sinus in the man's neck and pulled his head back to increase the flow of blood to the brain. Keio heard him groan. He then pried his fingernails under the nails of the man's first and second fingers, an ancient Oriental technique to revive a person who had fainted.

"Ow-wei!" the guard yelped. "Let go of me."

Rafael replied by thrusting the muzzle of a silenced Walther PPK into the man's face.

"Jesus," the sentry rasped. "You guys ain't cops. What is this shit? A *Kahka-roach?*"

"A cockroach?" McCarter snorted. "This guy's nuts."

"It's a pidgin expression for a rip-off," Rafael explained. "All the young studs who want to be cool in Hawaii speak pidgin. It's a bastard lingo with expressions from Hawaiian, English and any other language one wants to throw in."

"How do they understand each other?" Manning asked.

"They manage," the Cuban said with a shrug. "But our man better make himself understood now."

"You ask and I answer, mister," the guard replied, more than ready to spill his guts.

"Where is Oshimi holding Palmer?" Yakov demanded.

"Palmer?" the sentry said, frowning. "You mean the honkie they brought back from Japan?"

"Where is he?" Yakov insisted.

"Shit. I don't know. I'm just a little fish. They got him somewhere in the castle. . . ."

"How many men does Oshimi have in there?" Manning snapped.

"About fifty, I guess," the guard answered. "They're always moving guys in and out. Look, let me go and. . . ."

"And nothing," Rafael snorted.

The Cuban then put the guard into a deep sleep with the butt of the PPK.

The five-man army did not encounter any more guards in Land Cruisers. Oshimi's coffee fields were relatively small, and he had concentrated on using the field for cover. Security for the crops was limited.

When they reached the stone wall surrounding the castle, Phoenix Force discovered more sentries guarding the terrorist stronghold. Guards in bush shirts and khaki slacks patrolled the parade field on foot, each armed with a riot gun or a CAR-15 rifle.

Gary Manning attached a twelve-inch silencer to the barrel of his H&K G3 SG1. The special infrared telescopic sight was also mounted to the barrel of the gun.

Rafael Encizo adjusted the shoulder strap of his MP-5, sliding the weapon to his back, then he scaled the wall, its rocky surface offering plenty of hand- and footholds. The Cuban reached the top and scanned the parade field. He glanced down and saw a startled young Oriental face staring back at him.

Rafael immediately leaped from the wall, diving onto the guard before the terrorist could unsling a CAR from his shoulder. Both men fell to the ground. The Cuban pinned his opponent and hammered the butt of his Gerber Mark I into the sentry's forehead. Then he plunged the knife into the man's throat, slicing it open with a single stroke. Rafael rolled from his victim as blood gushed from the fatal wound.

A guard by the west wing of the castle saw the thrashing bodies near the wall and quickly unslung his weapon. His mouth opened to alert his comrades, unaware that Manning lay in a prone position on top of the wall—his sniper rifle held ready. The H&K SG1 hissed, and a 7.62mm round cut into the gun-cock's open mouth and popped out the back of his head.

McCarter and Katz scrambled over the wall and headed for the west wing, while Keio joined Rafael and moved to the east. Manning remained at the wall, scanning the area through his Starlite scope, finger ready on the H&K trigger.

Rafael and Keio jogged between a trio of cherry trees, the slender branches covered with white blossoms. They saw two shadows approach. The Cuban hit the dirt and assumed a prone position, his silenced Walther in his fist. Keio hid behind a narrow tree trunk, relying on shadows for concealment.

"Iras-shi," Keio called weakly. *"Isogimas, dozo."*

The sentries ran toward the trees to see what troubled their ''comrade.'' Rafael's PPK muttered a muffled snarl as he squeezed the trigger twice. Two .380-caliber rounds tagged one of the guards in the side of the head.

The man abruptly fell and his partner whirled, instantly spotting Rafael. Keio leaped forward and ripped the CAR-15 from the guard's grasp with a reverse roundhouse kick. A lightning fast *seiken* punch slammed into the man's midsection. Keio's other hand slashed a *shuto* stroke to his dazed opponent's collarbone, and then he finished him off with a *nukite* thrust. The tips of Ohara's fingers stabbed into the guard's solar plexus. The blow ruptured the man's intestines. He crumbled to the ground and died.

Yakov and McCarter had discovered three more sentries at the west wing. The guards desperately tried to unsling their weapons, but the silenced Uzi and Ingram harshly whispered death. Nine-millimeter projectiles tore into the trio, ripping flesh, muscle and organs.

Out of the corner of his eye, Yakov noticed a door

open. He turned to the entrance as a young gunman emerged with a .357 Colt Trooper in his fist. Before the Japanese slob could use his weapon, Yakov's hook-hand clamped around the man's wrist. The steel claws snapped shut like a bear trap, the pressure crunching bone and tearing cartilage from the wrist joint.

The big Magnum revolver fell from useless fingers as the savage opened his mouth to scream. Yakov's left arm lashed out in a cross-body stroke. The side of his hand struck the terrorist in the throat, crushing the thyroid cartilage and destroying the youth's windpipe. The Israeli released his opponent. The youth slumped, becoming a lifeless lump in the doorway.

"I think we've found a way inside the castle," Yakov called softly to McCarter.

PHOENIX FORCE CHECKED THE AREA for more sentries, but they had already dispatched the entire guard force on duty outside the castle. They would soon find out how many more lurked within. So far the assault had gone well, but Keio and Rafael had some bad news.

"We spotted a TV surveillance camera by the east wall," Rafael told the others.

"I followed the cables to a circuit breaker and used a magnesium-flare torch to short out the wiring," Keio added. "That ought to take care of the cameras stationed outside on that part of the building. Any other cameras may or may not be affected. It all depends on how they've got the system wired.''

"If there's only one camera," Manning said grimly, "you can bet there are others. Ten to one, we've already been picked up on a monitor."

"There's nothing we can do about that now," Yakov stated. "Except be prepared for trouble—*lots* of trouble."

"Maybe they didn't catch our act," Rafael commented. "We haven't heard any alarms, and there doesn't seem to be much activity inside the castle."

"They might have a silent alarm system," Keio warned. "They could be setting up a trap for us right now."

"Well," Yakov sighed, "we'll just have to take whatever they dish out and try to hit back even harder."

They entered the open door of Oshimi Castle.

The interior was a startling contrast to the building's pagoda-style exterior. Phoenix Force found themselves in a corridor with yellow tile floors, white walls and tube lights in the ceiling. The only furniture in the hallway consisted of a small metal desk and a chair. A sports magazine lay open on the desk top, and a telephone was mounted on the wall. The glass lens of a TV camera stared from its perch in a corner.

Yakov's Uzi sputtered fire through its silencer, and the camera burst into bits of plastic, metal and torn wires. The lack of electrical sparks suggested Keio's sabotage on the circuit breaker had put the entire monitor system out of order.

Footfalls on tile warned them someone was approaching. Yakov, McCarter and Encizo pressed their backs against one wall, while Keio and Manning crouched at the opposite side, weapons held ready. Shadows danced from a corner as the footsteps grew louder.

Three Orientals dressed in khaki uniforms appeared. Two men carried CARs and side arms. The third packed a pistol in a belt holster, but he carried a toolbox instead of a rifle.

The first man almost walked right into Yakov. The Israeli's Uzi quickly jammed into the JRC goon's weapon to prevent him from using the CAR. Yakov delivered a destructive uppercut to the guy's ribs, punching with the prosthetic hook. The terrorist doubled up, and Yakov's steel claw seized the man's neck in a vertebrae-crushing grip.

A three-round burst from McCarter's M-10 ripped open the handyman's chest and sent him hurtling into the nearest wall. Man and toolbox fell to the floor. The third JRC trooper prepared to fire his CAR-15 from the hip. Rafael's Walther PPK hissed, and a .380 round made a violent tunnel through the terrorist's forehead.

"Looks like they were sent to find and repair the short in the TV system," Keio remarked, nudging the toolbox with his boot.

"Then we haven't been detected yet," Manning sighed with relief.

"Don't count on it," McCarter snorted with typical cynicism.

They continued through the corridor until they discovered a thick steel door. Manning removed a block of plastic explosive from his field pack.

"Are you going to blow the door open?" Keio asked, concern in his voice.

"Why not?" Manning shrugged.

"Because that much C-4 will make a bloody great noise," McCarter said.

"This isn't C-4," the Canadian explained. "It's a potassium-chlorate compound with a gelatin buffer. Trust me."

The Phoenix Force demolitions expert tore off a small chunk of the gray putty substance and inserted it into the door's keyhole. He removed a pencil detonator and pressed it into the explosive.

"I'll set it for twenty seconds."

Phoenix Force moved a respectable distance from the door. The explosion resembled a whoosh more than a bang. The door creaked open, its entire lock mechanism blasted apart.

Manning and McCarter rushed to the door, while the others watched the corridor. The pair entered a short hallway. Glancing up, they noticed a thick steel net attached to the ceiling, extended from one wall to the next.

"Stun net," McCarter said. "Cops use them to handle violent felons like PCP junkies. It drops on a person, and a powerful electrical shock renders the victim immobile or unconscious."

"Can we walk under that thing without setting it off?" Manning asked.

"Only one way to find out," the Briton replied.

He moved forward quickly. Nothing happened. Manning followed. Further down the corridor, they found four unoccupied cells with barred doors. McCarter frowned when he saw the walls and ceilings of each cell were painted a soft shade of pink and the floors were covered by burgundy carpets. Instead of bunks, the cells featured large old-fashioned sofas.

"Oshimi must have an interior decorator on his penal staff," the Briton remarked.

"Color has an effect on one's personality and mood," Manning stated.

"I know," McCarter said with a grin. "I love it when a bird wears a bright red dress. Of course, basic black is nice too and...."

"You've got the right idea," Manning told him. "But color is used differently here. Tests on violent criminals and mental patients proved that pink makes one less aggressive. These cells have been designed to subtly break down a subject's resistance."

"Look there," McCarter declared, pointing at a small loudspeaker built into a cell wall. "How much do you want to bet they also pipe soft music into the cells? Elevator music, the type they use in hotels and shopping centers. Probably have subliminals slipped in to further weaken a prisoner's will."

"And there are air-conditioning vents in the cells," Manning added. "They can further relax a subject's resistance by pumping drug-laced air into the cells."

"But none of this would be enough to break a man

like Aaron Palmer into spilling his guts in less than...."

The sound of muffled shots burping from sound suppressors told McCarter and Manning their partners were in trouble. They dashed from the cell block to the outer corridor. The bullet-ravaged corpses of two uniformed terrorists were sprawled on the floor, but no member of Phoenix Force had even been scratched.

"A couple more wandering troopers," Yakov said. "They didn't seem to be expecting trouble."

"Still no organized action against us," Rafael added. "Find anything in there?"

"Plenty," Manning answered. "But no Palmer."

He and McCarter explained what they had found as Phoenix Force continued through the corridors. They reached a flight of stone steps. Cautiously, Manning, Yakov and McCarter ascended the stairs, weapons held ready. Keio and Rafael remained on the first floor and moved to another room.

Peering inside, they discovered three gasoline-powered generators with thick cables extending to the walls. Two men knelt by a circuit box, examining multicolored wires.

Rafael and Keio charged into the room. One of the terrorists raised his head in time to see the Cuban's boot swing forward. Rafael kicked him in the face hard, breaking teeth and bone. The JRC flunky fell to the floor, blood squirting from his broken nose.

The other terrorist sprang to his feet and clawed at a gun in a button-flap holster. Keio's hand lashed

out, the hard edge striking his opponent under the
heart. The blow knocked the man backward into a
wall. Ohara hit him under the jaw with a heel-of-the-
palm stroke and then drove a *nukite* hand under the
man's left ribs. He folded with a gasp, and Keio
shuto chopped him across the back of the neck, shattering vertebrae.

"They must still be looking for the short in the
TV system," Keio remarked, glancing over the machinery.

"That's better than them looking for us," Rafael
said. "This stuff looks ideal—let's sabotage the bastards."

"Can you tell anything from the wiring?" Rafael
asked.

"It's an independent job," Keio replied. "Which
means the wiring doesn't fit any customary pattern.
The generator cables are direct current lines. The
black cables on the wall are to the telephone system. I
recognize the blue wiring from the TV circuit breaker,
but I can only guess what the yellow, red and green
wires are."

"Alarm wires?" Rafael asked."

"At least one of them probably is," Keio answered. "But which one? If I had enough time to
examine the circuits, I could tell if there's a secon-
dary system and how it operates, and then I could
deactivate it. But by just cutting wires, there's a good
chance we'd set off an alarm."

"Is it safe to put the phones out of order?" Rafael
asked.

Keio nodded. "That'll reduce their ability to communicate. We'd better leave the rest be for now."

"Okay," Rafael agreed. "Let's wrap things up down here and find our amigos before the fireworks really start sizzling."

16

Colonel Yakov Katzenelenbogen led the way up the stone steps. Manning and McCarter followed. At the head of the stairs, the Israeli saw another uniformed terrorist patrolling a corridor. The sentry was a rather paunchy, young Japanese girl who had clipped her hair in a crew cut, robbing herself of any hope of being attractive.

Yakov raised his Uzi and squeezed the trigger. The phut-phut-phut of the silenced weapon was the girl's funeral dirge. Two bullets hit the female zealot in the chest, while the third 9mm slug tore into her throat. Blood splashed her bush shirt as she crumpled to the floor.

The ranks of international terrorism are usually comprised of young pseudointellectuals lured into the world of violence by the twisted scriptures of terrorist leaders. Many of these disciples of devastation are women. Gabriele Krocher, Shigenobu Fusako, Ulrike Meinhof and a thousand other female savages have proven to be as ruthless and vicious as their male counterparts.

Phoenix Force realized a terrorist is no longer a man or a woman. The fanatics of the modern tribes of terrorists are members of a different species. They are a hostile alien life form that must be stamped out if civilization is to survive. It *had* to be done, sure.

The three Phoenix Force members moved forward, scanning the corridor. They glanced up to see another steel net strung across the ceiling. The trio eyed the stun net with suspicion as they moved under it, approaching a wide metal door.

Suddenly the door slid open with an electric hum. A young Japanese, clad in a white laboratory smock, fearfully peered into the corridor. The snub-nose revolver in his fist weaved in his shaky grasp. His eyes expanded with horror when he saw the three warriors. Before he could use his .38, McCarter blasted apart the man's skull with a burst of Ingram rounds.

McCarter jogged to the door and glanced into the room. He saw computers, consoles, electrical graphs and plastic furniture. He also saw a pale-faced figure, dressed in a white smock, with a pistol held in both trembling hands.

McCarter dived to the floor and executed a fast shoulder roll across the tiles. The JRC lab boy's .32 automatic cracked. The small-caliber slug screeched against the steel doorframe. The terrorist tried to swing his pistol toward McCarter. Yakov's Uzi erupted, and 9mm projectiles zipped into the technician's chest. He fell to the floor, crimson stains appearing on his white smock.

Yakov entered the room in a low crouch. Dancing shadows on the wall warned him that more enemy technicians lurked in the lab. A Skorpion machine pistol snarled without benefit of a silencer. The spray of 7.65mm rounds ricocheted against the wall above Yakov's head as the gunman opened fire from the cover of a computer printout machine. Manning aimed his H&K SG1 around the doorway and squeezed the trigger. The JRC machine gunner's head popped from the impact of a flat-nosed bullet cutting through the bridge of his nose into his skull.

"Don't shoot," Professor Ouzu Yoichi cried, thrusting his hands into the air.

"Watch the hall," Yakov shouted, training his Uzi on the Japanese scientist.

"Got it," Manning replied. He had entered the lab and hastily slipped out of his field pack, placing the bag of explosives on the floor.

The Israeli approached Ouzu, while McCarter quickly checked the lab for any adversaries who might be hiding behind equipment. Yakov stepped around a monitor consul.

He found Aaron Palmer.

The deputy director of the CIA was strapped to a metal chair. Electrodes were clamped to his shaven head, wires extending to the console set.

"What have you done to him?" Yakov demanded, thrusting the Uzi at Yoichi.

"He is merely asleep," the scientist replied. "We haven't harmed him."

"What is this?" the Israeli insisted. "What are you doing here?"

"It's an electroencephalograph with a few *modifications*," Ouzu explained.

"What sort of modifications?" Yakov asked.

"We've got company," Manning announced.

Four armed terrorists had appeared at the end of the hall. The Canadian's H&K hissed twice and two men fell. The others retreated around a corner.

"Better save the questions for later," McCarter urged. He hurried to join Manning at the door.

"We came here for the answers," Yakov replied stubbornly. "I'll be with you in a minute."

Yakov glared at Yoichi. "What modifications?"

"An electroencephalograph records an EEG reading—an electroencephalogram," the scientist began, speaking slowly, stalling for time. "This is, in layman's terms, a method of reading the fluctuations of the brain. The brain waves—alpha, beta, delta and theta waves, to be exact."

"You mean this machine can read minds?" Yakov frowned.

"Essentially," Yoichi confirmed. "The science of electroencephalography dates back to Canton in 1875. Hans Berger made the first big breakthrough with the EEG galvanometer in 1924. Now I've taken the science to a new peak."

Yoichi turned and pointed at the console. "This receives the EEG readings, like a galvanometer does, but it's connected to the memory banks of a computer that translates the brain waves into words. This is a remarkable advance, but I've taken the process even further."

Gunfire roared from the corridor. Terrorists had appeared at both ends of the hallway. McCarter and Manning opened fire on the inexperienced JRC troops, mowing down half a dozen of them and forcing the others to seek cover. The terrorists shot back, armed with an assortment of full and semiauto weapons.

"I've invented an electroencephalo stimulator," Yoichi continued. "I call it an EES machine. It creates and relays brain waves to a subject. This serves as a direct command to the brain—affecting conscious and subconscious thought. It stimulates the brain to think of whatever subject is inserted into the EES. The natural brain waves of information on the subject are then picked up by the electrodes and fed into my advanced EEG and translated into the computer that prints all the data into the external disk-drive units. This is then printed into a series of diskettes—computer cassettes."

"So this is how you bastards drained information from your victims," Yakov said in a cold flat voice. "How many of these monster machines do you people have?"

"This is the only one of its kind in the world," Yoichi replied. "We kept it at a base in Kyoto until we decided to transport everything here for additional security...."

A team of terrorists at the end of the corridor had set up an M-60 machine gun, mounted on a bipod. Manning and McCarter lobbed grenades at the JRC hit team. The terrorists scrambled, some trying to grab the grenades to hurl them back at the defenders, the others just trying to flee before the explosions occurred. Both efforts were in vain. The grenades erupted. Mangled bodies and twisted metal were scattered all over the hallway.

"What happened to the other men who have had their minds tapped by this computerized freak?" Yakov demanded.

"The EES is not a freak," Yoichi replied stiffly. "The previous subjects had to be terminated of course."

"It would be a pleasure to terminate you," the Israeli told him. "So don't tempt me. Unhook Aaron from this contraption."

The scientist slowly lowered his arms.

Yoichi moved to the deputy director and stepped behind the chair. He slipped his right hand into the pocket of his smock and slowly drew a .25-caliber Raven automatic. Yoichi raised the tiny pistol and thumbed off the safety catch.

Yakov had expected such a move. Aware that the Uzi is an indiscriminate weapon, designed for rapid fire at close quarters, not precision shooting, he had already released the machine gun and drawn the Colt Commander from shoulder leather. The big .45 auto bellowed and a 185-grain, jacketed hollowpoint round blasted Professor Yoichi's face into scarlet pulp. The scientist crashed to the floor in a twitching heap.

"Guess you finally got tired of chatting with that bastard," McCarter remarked.

Manning jogged across the room to Palmer, while Yakov joined McCarter at the doorway. Katz glanced at the corridor. Bloodstains were everywhere—the walls, the floor, even the ceiling. Mangled metal lay among the bodies of slain JRC terrorists.

"They've got a taste of first-rate arse kicking," McCarter told Yakov. "The bastards aren't really trained for combat, but you can't call this lot cowards. They'll be back just as soon as they think up a new strategy."

"If they've got grenades, they'll be able to toss plenty of them at our position from both ends of the hall," the Israeli remarked.

"I'm sure they've got grenades," McCarter said. "They've got everything else. My guess is they haven't used explosives because they don't want to damage any of this mad-scientist equipment. Still, if I was in command, I'd order them to use grenades and worry about the damage later."

"Or they might pump tear gas or nerve gas through the air-conditioning vents," Yakov added, "if they decide the doctor is expendable or figure we've killed him anyway."

"Should we make a run for it?" the Englishman asked.

"We can't stay here," Yakov replied. "Any sign of Rafael or Keio?"

"No," McCarter frowned, concern forming deep lines in his brow. "Not yet."

Manning joined them. Aaron Palmer's unconscious body was slung over his shoulder. The Canadian carried the CIA man as easily as one might haul a knapsack.

"What are we going to do with this guy?" he asked.

"We'll figure that out after we get out of this death trap," Yakov said.

"Are we heading upstairs or down?" McCarter inquired, gathering up Manning's field pack.

"Down," the Israeli said. "Our partners might need help. Besides, the cell block might be the safest place to leave Aaron."

"Concentrate on covering me as much as you can," Manning urged. "I won't be able to shoot very well while I'm carrying our friend."

"Let's go," Katz said.

McCarter slipped out the door first, his Ingram aimed at the stairwell. Manning followed. Yakov came out last, Uzi braced across his steel arm and pointed at the opposite end of the corridor.

None of the Phoenix Force members noticed the slight click from overhead, their ears still ringing from the earlier gunfire and explosions. A shadow fell across them, and they glanced up to see the steel net dropping from the ceiling.

"Oh, shit," McCarter snarled as he tried to dodge the net.

His curse became a scream of agony as electricity coursed through the stun net, delivering a violent shock to all four men. Yakov was especially vulnerable because of his prosthetic arm, which is highly conductive to electricity. The Israeli trembled helplessly under the net.

McCarter angrily thrashed and cursed, unable to break free of the paralyzing grip of the stun net. Palmer's unconscious body merely twitched under the assault. Manning clenched his teeth and slowly crawled beneath the electric steel cables, but even his great strength was drained by the relentless voltage of the stun net.

Suddenly the net was yanked away by rubber-gloved hands. Manning stared up into the muzzles of several weapons. The hall was now full of JRC terrorists. A tall muscular Oriental, with a stern stony face, stared down at Manning, his black eyes ablaze with rage.

"*Oki-mas,*" Daito-*san* hissed.

Manning slowly rose. He did not resist as terrorists took his weapons. The Canadian's muscles were still too numb to fight. The JRC goons also knelt by the dazed bodies of McCarter and Yakov to disarm them.

"*Amerika-jin, butah,*" Daito spat as he reached for the hilt of a weapon thrust through the red sash bound around his lean waist.

The *iai-jutsu* draw happened so fast, Manning barely caught a glimpse of the two-and-a-half-foot-long blade when it cleared the scabbard. The Canadian stared at the weapon in disbelief. It was a *katana*—the two-handed fighting sword of a samurai.

"Jesus," Manning muttered as Daito raised the weapon overhead.

He tried to move away, but his legs buckled, and

he fell to his knees before the feet of the sword-wielding terrorist. Daito-*san* chuckled in ruthless amusement. He stepped forward, the *katana* held high, prepared to decapitate Manning with a single swift stroke.

"Ee-ya," a voice ordered sharply.

Daito froze, the weapon still poised to strike. Everyone turned to see Professor Edward Oshimi marching toward the captives. His stride was arrogant, confident. Oshimi was a *daimyo* warlord in his castle. An absolute monarch and tyrant who held the power of life and death within his kingdom.

"Ee-ya, Daito-*san,"* he repeated. *"Matteh, doshi. Matteh."*

"Hai, Oshimi-*sama,"* Daito replied, returning his sword to its scabbard.

"We mustn't kill our guests," Oshimi said with a cold smile. "Not until we've shown them how truly bitter defeat can be."

"You mean it gets worse?" McCarter groaned weakly.

17

Surrounded by a dozen armed terrorists, Katz, Manning and McCarter were escorted up the next flight of stairs. Two terrorists shared the chore of carrying Aaron Palmer. Professor Oshimi led the group. He seemed to have little concern about the men he had lost in the firefight and elected to act as a tour guide for his prisoners.

"Here," he announced at the head of the stairs. "Here is something beyond your ability to understand...culture."

The third floor of the castle resembled a shopping mall that specialized in Japanese restaurants and Oriental curio shops. Sliding doors with bamboo frames and ornately painted silk screens were positioned on both sides of the hall. Cherry blossoms with Mount Fuji in the background were painted on one door. Another door featured a *daimyo* mounted on horseback, leading his samurai troops into battle. A third depicted a swordsman fighting a serpentine dragon.

"These rooms are a small piece of the greatest civilization in history," Oshimi declared. "A civilization the Western powers have tried to destroy. Your people pushed Japan into a war it could not win so you could justify the occupation of my country. You tried to corrupt it and turn it into a serfdom under the command of the United States.''

None of the three members of Phoenix Force made any comment to these accusations. They knew the man who held them captive was totally insane.

''Here we have a geisha house,'' Oshimi continued, pointing at the colorful sliding doors. ''A Shinto temple and a dojo. Perhaps, I should say the dojo of Daito-*san*.''

The stone-faced Japanese swordsman's chest expanded when he heard his name mentioned by his master. Oshimi smiled at Daito.

''Magnificent, isn't he?'' Oshimi said. ''A twentieth-century samurai. The last of his kind. A living tribute to the Code of Bushido. But he will train others, and the great tradition of the knight warriors of Japan will continue.''

''How does all this glory of Japan's lost past go hand in hand with terrorism and that computerized inquisition device downstairs?'' Yakov asked dryly.

''Terrorism? Inquisition?'' Oshimi raised his eyebrows. ''We're liberators of our nation. Any methods we use are justified by that goal.''

''Your nation?'' McCarter sneered. ''You seem to forget you're an American, Oshimi.''

The madman's eyes bulged from their sockets. ''I am not an American.''

''That's right,'' Manning agreed. ''You rejected your country. Guess you're just a traitor.''

"I returned to my people," Oshimi declared. "I am Japanese."

"And that's why you've slaughtered so many of 'your people'—to liberate them?" Yakov remarked.

"I'm tempted to kill all of you right here and now," Oshimi rasped, "but that would deny me the pleasure of having my enemies witness my greatest victory."

The congregation mounted another flight of stone steps to the fourth story at the summit of the castle. The "penthouse" consisted of a single large room. It was the headquarters of the Japanese Red Cell and the brain center of Oshimi's evil plans.

They entered the war room, which was filled with computers, maps and control consoles. Two terrorists dropped the unconscious Aaron Palmer onto one of several plastic chairs that surrounded a huge circular conference table. The ceiling extended into a great concave thirty feet high—the dome of Oshimi's rooftop observatory. A telescope was mounted directly under the dome.

"Ah, Mr. Palmer," Oshimi declared when he heard the CIA man groan as he began to regain consciousness. "I'm so glad you're going to be able to see this."

The evil genius consulted a digital clock on the wall. "Two-fifty," he announced. "Ten minutes from now, we shall all witness the beginning of a new era—the New Empire of Japan!"

"Excuse me, your lordship," McCarter said with contempt. "But I'm a bit confused. You want to be the bloody king of Japan, but you're the head of the Red Cell—which suggests your followers are commies or at least Marxists. How do you work out this difference in politics?"

"The New Empire will establish a Marxist-socialist government," Oshimi replied. "And strengthen Japan's ties with the Soviet Union, Mainland China and other Communist nations. We'll still do business with the West, but to a very limited degree. Thus, we'll avoid contamination from the United States and its boot-licking allies."

"What about contamination from the Communists?" Yakov asked. "Or do you really believe they're trustworthy?"

"Hardly," Oshimi replied, smiling. "I'm well aware of the gangster mentality of the Kremlin. If we allow the Soviets to send in their military and the KGB, they would try to turn us into a satellite country like North Korea. We'll accept their technology, weaponry and other materials, but we won't let them send troops or advisors."

"Why should the Russians agree to your terms?" Manning asked.

"Because we have something to bargain with," Oshimi answered. "Advanced technology that the Soviets will want badly enough to agree to our conditions."

"Your brain-draining machine?" Yakov said grimly.

"Indeed," Oshimi confirmed. "Of course, we won't tell them everything. First, we'll sell the Russians information extracted from Mr. Palmer. You killed Professor Yoichi, but not before we had a chance to tap a considerable amount of top-secret data from our guest.''

"Why would Moscow believe you?" McCarter asked.

"They'll see the proof for themselves," Oshimi declared. "The whole world will talk about the greatest naval disaster in history."

"What the hell are you talking about?" Manning demanded.

Oshimi walked to a control panel under the observatory dome and pressed a button. The dome slowly parted. Oshimi pushed another button. A section of the floor slowly began to sink out of view, taking the telescope with it.

"I imagine you people have read some of the government files about me," Oshimi remarked as he pressed more buttons. "You may have wondered why I moved to Hawaii instead of Japan. The reason is, I needed an isolated headquarters located between Japan and the U.S. mainland. Also, the Hawaiian Islands offered the perfect site for my demonstration of power."

The hydraulic lift under the war room hummed as a large tubular device with a block-shaped base rose from the floor to replace the telescope. Oshimi placed his hand on the contraption and smiled.

"This," he said, "is a laser cannon—actually a particle-beam projector. It's a vast improvement of the weapon I offered the U.S. government over a decade ago. This cannon has a range of almost forty thousand miles. Not much compared to the range of nuclear missiles these days, but it suits my needs.''

Aaron Palmer groaned as his head began to clear. "Where am I?"

"I'll explain later," Oshimi assured him. "But first I want to thank you for telling me the coordinates of the route of the USS *Zesus*."

Palmer stared at him with astonished horror. "How...?"

"What is the USS *Zesus*?" Yakov asked.

The Israeli wanted to stall for time. Rafael and Keio had not been captured...if they were still alive....

"The *Zesus* is a nuclear submarine," Oshimi explained. "It is currently docked at the Na Pali Coast of Kauai. The U.S. Navy Pacific Missile Range is located there at Barking Sands. The *Zesus* leaves at 0300 hours on a clandestine mission to the Philippines."

Oshimi turned to the controls and pushed a lever forward. "But that voyage will be interrupted," he announced. "The laser cannon has been programmed to see to that, thanks to a computer diskette inserted into the control console. A sonar tracking device in Kauai will transmit a signal when the *Zesus* is on target. That will trigger my cannon...."

"For God's sake," Palmer cried. "There are more than two hundred men on board that submarine."

"And nothing can save them now," Oshimi declared. "The process operating the cannon is irreversible. It is impossible to stop it."

"What about missiles on the sub?" Yakov asked. "If you detonate them, you'll destroy all of the Hawaiian Islands...including yourself."

"Surely you know better than that," Oshimi sighed. "Sinking the submarine won't detonate the missiles. There may be a radiation leak, but that won't concern us."

"If you blow up that sub," McCarter said, "about a hundred U.S. fighter jets will blast this castle to bits within an hour."

"How will they know I'm responsible?" the madman asked. "The particle beam is invisible. It is basically just a concentrated ray of light that cannot be detected or traced by radar. Who would suspect the owner of a coffee plantation of such a deed? Or that my observatory conceals a secret weapon?"

"You couldn't have prepared all this in less than a day," Manning remarked, also trying to stall for time.

"Of course not," Oshimi nodded. "I've prepared for years. With so many military installations in the Hawaiian Islands, I knew one day a proper target would arrive. Besides, this will be the heart of the first sovereign territory of the Empire of Japan."

"You think you can blackmail the United States into giving you the Hawaiian Islands?" McCarter laughed. "Jesus, you're bloody nuts."

"All great men of vision have been called mad,"

Oshimi replied. "Alexander, Caesar—both succeeded where lesser men failed. Besides, America is not the fearsome giant it once was. They surrendered the Panama Canal to General Torrijos. Wasn't that blackmail? They backed down from the challenge of the hostage situation in Iran. A paper tiger, that is the United States. I do not fear it."

Oshimi added, "If it is not my karma to reclaim Japan's glory and build a new empire in this lifetime, I am prepared to die or take my own life. You see, I believe in Shintoism, the religion of my ancestors. I will be reborn in another life and continue my destiny until I succeed."

"Now I've heard everything," McCarter muttered. "A born-again lunatic."

Suddenly a loud buzz sang from the console. The screen of a sonar tracking monitor revealed a blob of light that slowly approached the center of a bull's-eye.

"The *Zesus* is on schedule," Oshimi declared. "You can watch its progress on the sonar screen. When it reaches the center, the cannon will fire a single burst of incredible energy that will cut through the steel hull of the most advanced submarine in the world, as though it were made of papier-mâché."

"At least this guy will get his when Randisi hits the castle at 0500 hours," Manning whispered to Yakov.

"We're not dead yet," the Israeli replied, trying to judge the odds of jumping the closest JRC gunman who stood guard over the Phoenix Force trio.

"Enjoy the program, gentlemen," Oshimi laughed. "It will be the last thing you'll ever see."

He raised his head and gazed up at the night sky beyond the muzzle of the laser cannon.

18

"No!" Professor Edward Oshimi screamed when he saw the figure positioned between the open doors of the observatory dome.

Rafael Encizo aimed his H&K MP-5 at the horrified terrorist leader. He squeezed the trigger. A spray of 9mm projectiles smashed into Oshimi's face. Bullets chopped through teeth and bone. Eyeballs exploded in their sockets. Professor Edward Oshimi's skull vanished in a nova of splattered brains and skull fragments.

Japanese Red Cell terrorists gasped in astonishment as they watched their messiah's decapitated corpse crumple to the floor. Rafael hosed two of the JRC underlings with 9mm rounds. The bullet-riddled zealots staggered and fell as their comrades swung weapons toward the observatory and opened fire.

They reacted too slowly. Rafael had already retreated behind the thick arch of the dome. The surviving terrorists were too busy trying to waste the Cuban to notice the tall silent figure who crept through the door of the war room.

A JRC trooper stationed by the door screamed. A long blood-drenched object burst from the center of his chest. Keio Ohara had driven the blade of his *wakazashi* clean through his victim from behind. Another terrorist turned to see the Colt 1911A1 in Keio's left fist. The pistol roared, and another JRC fanatic bought death when a .45 slug penetrated his heart.

Yakov, Manning and McCarter had already leaped into action like a trio of wildcats. Reacting the moment Rafael provided a distraction, the three warriors instantly turned on their captors.

Manning's technique was simple and effective. He grabbed a JRC guard's CAR-15 in one hand and yanked the barrel toward the ceiling while he punched the startled terrorist in the mouth. The powerful Canadian easily wrenched the Colt automatic rifle from his dazed opponent and dropped to one knee. Three 5.5mm rounds terminated the worldly cares of the fellow he had punched out. A second volley of bullets tagged another JRC goon before he could draw a side arm. The man's body was propelled into the base of the laser cannon. He slumped against the superweapon and died before he could whisper *sayonara*.

David McCarter *shuto*-chopped a .357 S&W from a terrorist's grasp. He followed with a combination back fist to the man's right temple and a knee to the groin. The devastated terrorist wilted to the floor as McCarter scooped up the discarded Magnum revolver.

He aimed the .357 at another terrorist who had fled to the cover of a computer console. The S&W

roared, and a 158-grain wadcutter drilled a vicious path that started under the guy's left shoulder blade, ripped through his heart and emerged at the left breast pocket of his uniform shirt.

Yakov Katzenelenbogen pounced on a JRC sentry. Both men crashed to the floor and struggled over ownership of the guard's Skorpion machine pistol. Yakov ended the wrestling match by ripping out his opponent's throat with the steel hook.

Two unarmed technicians dashed for the collection of Phoenix Force weapons on the conference table.

Then hell struck from all sides. Manning swung the CAR-15 at the JRC tech men. Yakov, in a prone position, braced the Skorpion across his prosthetic arm and opened fire. Keio had returned his *wakazashi* to its scabbard and held the blazing .45 in both hands. More than a dozen projectiles in three different calibers pumped into the terrorist technicians. The impact sent their bullet-shredded bodies hurtling over the tabletop. As they tumbled across the furniture, Rafael sprayed the pair with a salvo of 9mm H&K rounds before the butchered corpses crashed to the floor.

"Damn," McCarter shouted, firing a hasty shot with the Magnum as a terrorist escaped out the door.

The .357 slug rang sourly when it struck the steel frame of the doorway. Keio bolted after the fleeing terrorist, followed by a furious McCarter.

Manning ran to the control panel of the laser cannon, while Yakov helped the drug-sedated Palmer to his feet. Rafael jumped from his perch, caught the barrel of the laser gun and swung down to the floor like a trapeze artist. The Cuban's warm smile vanished when he saw the concern on his partners' faces.

"A nuclear sub is about to be blasted out of the water," Manning updated him, hopelessly trying to make sense out of the maze of buttons, switches and knobs on the panel. "And I'll be damned if I can see how we can stop it!"

The white blob on the sonar screen continued to move closer to the bull's-eye. . . .

Keio and McCarter recognized Daito-*san* as they chased the terrorist swordsman down the stairwell. Daito jumped down the last six steps at the very moment the two Phoenix Force members opened fire. Bullets hissed behind the hurtling figure and ricocheted against stone.

Daito hit the floor in a *mae ukemi* roll. McCarter and Keio reached the foot of the stairs in time to see their quarry charge through one of the sliding doors. Flimsy bamboo shattered and silk screens tore as Daito plunged into the room.

"What's he up to?" McCarter wondered aloud as he and Keio cautiously approached the damaged door.

"*Nihon-jin!*" Daito called from inside the room. "*Anatah-no o-namae wah?*"

"I am Ohara Keio," Keio replied in Japanese, using the traditional style of putting the family name first.

"You carry a sword, Ohara-*san*," Daito declared.

"I too have a *wakazashi*. Come fight me. Blade against blade, on equal terms."

Keio did not have to consider the challenge. "I accept, Daito-*san*."

"I will trust you to honor the Code of Bushido."

"And I will trust you."

Keio handed his pistol and Ingram M-10 to McCarter as he explained the conversation to the confused Briton.

"Jesus, Keio," McCarter said. "That son of a bitch is a terrorist. His word isn't worth shit."

"He knows he is about to die," Ohara stated. "And he wants to die as a samurai. I think he's telling the truth about that.

"Keep out of this duel, David," Keio told him. "This is between Daito and me. I want to finish him off."

"All right," McCarter reluctantly agreed. "If you lose I'm not about to agree to a sword fight with that bastard. I'll just shoot his bloody head off."

Ohara shoved open the sliding door. The room within was a dojo, almost identical to the Zembu Dojo in Tokyo. The floors were hardwood, and an assortment of Oriental weapons hung on the walls. Daito-*san* stood in the center of the room and bowed. Keio returned the gesture.

The JRC zealot had kept his word. His *katana* had been placed on a black wood stand, and he was armed with a samurai short sword.

"You are brave Ohara-*san*," Daito declared as Keio entered the dojo. "I will try to kill you quickly."

Then he charged, slashing his sword at Keio's wrist, hoping to disable Ohara before he could even draw his weapon.

Keio pivoted and executed a flawless *iai-jutsu* draw, his sword streaking from its scabbard to block the attack with a clang of metal on metal. Daito hopped back, seized his sword with both hands and delivered a lightning-fast series of cuts and thrusts. Keio's *wakazashi* moved just as fast, blocking and parrying every stroke.

Daito smoothly changed tactics. He swung an overhead slash, then altered the attack to a lunge, trying to stab Keio in the throat with the slanted point of his *wakazashi*. The Phoenix Force member stepped back and met the sword thrust with his own weapon. Daito's left arm suddenly struck out, stamping the heel of his palm into the side of Ohara's head.

The blow staggered Keio. He nearly lost his balance as Daito rushed in, prepared to deliver a killing stroke with the sword. Keio's blade flashed. Metal sang once more. Keio's leg shot out in a rapid side kick, driving a foot into Daito's abdomen.

The kick sent Daito hurtling backward. He fell against the sword stand. Enraged, the terrorist unexpectedly threw his *wakazashi* at Ohara. Keio easily dodged the sword.

Daito whirled away from the stand, moving with the grace of a dancer and the speed of a whirlwind. Keio barely saw the blur of metallic light that extended from the swordman's fists. Daito had drawn his *katana* from its place in the stand.

Unprepared to deal with the longer samurai sword, Keio was caught off guard. The *katana* struck with tremendous force, the stroke powered by Daito's entire body and the momentum of his attack. Blade met blade. Keio's *wakazashi* popped out of his hand.

Daito instantly turned to deliver a decapitating stroke aimed at the side of Keio's neck. Keio avoided the sword by suddenly collapsing to the floor. The tactic surprised Daito, who found his *katana* cutting nothing but air.

For a flickering of a second, Daito was not certain what had happened. Keio, sprawled on the floor in front of Daito, did not hesitate. Pivoting on the small of his back, he threw a reverse roundhouse kick, his foot striking the flat of Daito's sword. The terrorist half turned, managing to hold on to his weapon. Ohara's other leg powered a second kick. The edge of his boot hit Daito under the rib cage.

The JRC swordsman groaned in pain and surprise. He stumbled backward, lashing a wild sweep with his *katana* to keep Keio from closing in. Keio, however, rolled away from his adversary and sprang to his feet, quickly seizing a *boken* from the wall. Daito scoffed as he watched Keio Ohara prepare to defend himself with a wooden practice sword.

David McCarter aimed his .357 Magnum at the terrorist. Code of Bushido, be damned, he thought.

But the Briton hesitated and did not squeeze the trigger. He had given his word to Keio.

Daito slashed a powerful *shomin-uchi* overhead stroke. The *boken* whacked into the flat of Daito's sword, then it swung in a fast arc and slammed into the terrorist's left deltoid muscle.

Startled by the blow to his shoulder, Daito retreated, spun sharply and launched another *shominuchi*. Keio stepped forward. He suddenly bent at the knees and raised his *boken* and turned slightly. The wooden shaft struck Daito's forearms, but the terrorist still retained his *katana*.

Keio had pivoted under the raised swords to place himself beside Daito. He quickly seized the "blade" of his *boken* and rammed the butt of the wooden handle into his adversary's stomach. Daito doubled up with a grunt, and Keio immediately swung his *boken* at the base of the terrorist's skull. He missed the mark, striking Daito across the shoulder blades.

Daito bellowed with rage and scrambled away before Keio could deliver another stroke. Both men swung their weapons once more. Keio tried to strike the flat of the *katana*, aware that the steel, although incredibly sharp, is relatively brittle. Daito turned his blade slightly and the razor edge met wood.

The *katana* sliced through the *boken* as if it was a breadstick. Keio suddenly found himself holding a foot-long piece of wood that had been cleanly cut by a diagonal sword stroke.

A cry of victory sprang from Daito's throat as he executed a cross-body slash at Ohara's neck. Keio dropped to one knee, ducking beneath the whirling steel blade. His arms lunged forward. Daito screamed and staggered backward, the *katana* falling from his open fingers.

Keio Ohara had rammed the splintered point of his severed *boken* into his opponent's solar plexus.

Daito's mouth opened and bloodied vomit poured from it. His eyes opened wide in disbelief as his fingers explored the stump of wood buried in his chest. The upward thrust of the *boken* stroke had driven the tip into the terrorist's heart. Daito stared at Keio, blinked once and fell to the floor—dead.

"How much time is left?" Aaron Palmer asked.

"Two minutes," Rafael Encizo replied, watching the sonar screen. "Three at the most."

"Gary," Yakov began, "have you been able to determine how the laser cannon operates?"

"Hell," the Canadian answered as he scanned the controls, "this is out of my league. Maybe Keio could figure this thing out."

"There isn't time," Palmer insisted. "Can't we just push every button and throw every switch?"

"It won't do any good," Yakov answered. "The entire system is automated. The computer programming can't be reversed."

"But we can't just stand by and let it blast the *Zesus* out of the water," the CIA man exclaimed.

"If we can't deactivate it," Rafael said, "then there's only one thing left to do...."

"Destroy it," Manning confirmed.

He ran to the conference table and grabbed his field pack full of explosives. The Canadian extracted a package wrapped in brown wax paper—a pound block of C-4 plastic explosives.

"I've got enough here to blow up the cannon," he announced. "As a matter of fact, this entire room is going up in smoke."

"Will it work?" Palmer inquired.

"Hell," Rafael said, "the laser cannon can't fire if it doesn't exist anymore."

"Undeniable logic," Yakov agreed, glancing at the sonar screen. "You've got less than a minute, Gary."

The Canadian inserted a special blasting cap into the doughlike substance.

"You're down to thirty-five seconds now," Katz said.

"And I've set the detonator for thirty," Manning told them. "Let's get the hell out of here."

The four men bolted from the room and dashed for the stairs. They nearly ran into Keio and McCarter who were heading up the steps. There was no time to explain, as Manning and Rafael grabbed their partners by the arms and led them down the stairs. They reached the third floor and immediately ran to the next flight of stairs.

They were halfway down the steps to the second floor when the explosion occurred.

The observatory dome broke apart like an eggshell. The walls of the war room split open, and machinery erupted, severing wires and cables. The floor gave way, and the entire fourth floor crashed down into the third. Almost a ton of flaming, twisted rubble filled the corridor. Oshimi's "little Japan" section was crushed by the wreckage.

The whole castle trembled from the explosion.

Phoenix Force and Aaron Palmer were thrown off balance and toppled down the stairs to the second floor. A cloud of dust and smoke floated from the ruined stories above. Gary Manning shook his head to clear it and glanced at his watch.

"Seven seconds to spare," he announced. "We did it!"

EPILOGUE

The five men of Phoenix Force and Deputy Director Palmer watched the Bell UH-1D gunship from the boundaries of the coffee plantation as the helicopter hovered over the remnants of Oshimi Castle.

"I've got the place on target," Lieutenant Randisi declared.

"Do it," Yakov spoke into the handset of the field radio in their jeep.

"Yes, sir," Randisi replied.

Two missiles streaked from the undercarriage of the chopper. The projectiles sailed into the castle. Thermite-charged warheads exploded, and the entire structure burst apart. Flames rose from the wreckage as another pair of missiles flew into the debris.

"That did it, sir," Randisi announced. "Target destroyed. Terminated with extra prejudice."

"Good work, Lieutenant," Yakov said. "Return to Keahole Airport. We'll meet you there."

The Israeli switched off the field radio and turned to his fellow members of Phoenix Force. "It's over," he smiled weakly.

"I don't see why you insisted on destroying the castle," Palmer said. "The laser cannon was put out of action, the submarine was saved and all of Oshimi's men are dead."

"You would have liked to get your hands on that EES machine, eh?" McCarter commented.

"A device like that should have been turned over to our government," Palmer said.

"It doesn't exist anymore," Rafael stated. "The United States won't get it and neither will the Russians."

"We could have used the EES machine to question enemy agents," Palmer said. "And to make completely foolproof security checks of personnel and defectors from behind the Iron Curtain. It could serve as a perfect lie detector. . . ."

"Professor Yoichi's advancements in electroencephalography exceeded anything previously accomplished in the field," Manning remarked. "What could that lead to? Not only extracting information but also programming subjects by stimulating fluctuations of the brain?"

"The ability to turn people into robots," Keio added. "No government should be able to wield that kind of power."

Yakov shrugged. "For now, all that matters is that we've accomplished our mission. It's time to go home."

PHOENIX FORCE

AN EXECUTIONER SERIES

#8 Aswan Hellbox

MORE GREAT ACTION
COMING SOON!

Jeremiah Blackwell had a dream. He was going to be
King of Africa. But first he had to amass the money
and tactical support. That was where the Communists
came in.

They were prepared to pay a fortune for an act of
destruction that would plunge the Middle East into
chaos. Blackwell had just such an act already
planned. He would destroy Egypt's Aswan High
Dam.

The mighty structure, one of the wonders of the
modern world, was horrifyingly vulnerable to his
rockets and 300 fanatical assault troops.

But the free world has shock troops of its own—
Phoenix Force! Only unspeakable catastrophe can
stop America's five-man army.... Will the fire-
blazing force finally meet its match?

HE'S EXPLOSIVE.
HE'S UNSTOPPABLE.
HE'S MACK BOLAN!

e learned his deadly skills in Vietnam…then put them to use by destroying
e Mafia in a blazing one-man war. Now **Mack Bolan** is back to battle new
reats to freedom, the enemies of justice and democracy—and he's recruited
ome high-powered combat teams to help. **Able Team**—Bolan's famous Death
quad, now reborn to tackle urban savagery too vicious for regular law
nforcement. And **Phoenix Force**—five extraordinary warriors handpicked
y Bolan to fight the dirtiest of anti-terrorist wars around the world.

Fight alongside these three courageous forces for freedom in all-new,
ulse-pounding action-adventure novels! Travel to the jungles of South America,
e scorching sands of the Sahara and the desolate mountains of Turkey,
nd feel the pressure and excitement building page after page, with nonstop
ction that keeps you enthralled until the explosive conclusion! Yes, Mack Bolan
nd his combat teams are living large…and they'll fight against all odds to
rotect our way of life!

ow you can have all the new Executioner novels delivered right to our home!

ou won't want to miss a single one of these exciting new action-adventures.
nd you don't have to! Just fill out and mail the coupon following and we'll enter
our name in the Executioner home subscription plan. You'll then receive
ur brand-new action-packed books in the Executioner series every other
onth, delivered right to your home! You'll get two **Mack Bolan** novels, one
ble Team and one **Phoenix Force.** No need to worry about sellouts at
e bookstore…you'll receive the latest books by mail as soon as they come off
e presses. That's four enthralling action novels every other month, featuring all
ree of the exciting series included in The Executioner library. Mail the card
day to start your adventure.

REE! Mack Bolan bumper sticker.

hen we receive your card we'll send your four explosive Executioner
ovels and, absolutely FREE, a Mack Bolan "Live Large" bumper sticker! This
rge, colorful bumper sticker will look great on your car, your bulletin board, or
nywhere else you want people to know that you like to "Live Large." And you are
nder no obligation to buy anything—because your first four books come on a
-day free trial! If you're not thrilled with these four exciting books, just return
em to us and you'll owe nothing. The bumper sticker is yours to keep. FREE!

Don't miss a single one of these thrilling novels…mail the card now, while
u're thinking about it. And get the Mack Bolan bumper sticker FREE!

BOLAN FIGHTS AGAINST ALL ODDS TO DEFEND FREEDOM!

Mail this coupon today!